Tilly was hazi̇... what she was doing was very dangerous.

That *Silas* was very dangerous. But the room was so cold that it seemed to be numbing her ability to respond and react in a normal way. And Silas felt so warm lying on top of her, compelling her to arch up to him, wanting something much more intimate.

She shuddered with pleasure when he spread his fingers against her scalp and held her head while he plundered her mouth with the intimate thrust of his tongue until she was in the grip of the most intense physical longing she had ever experienced.

The shock of her own sexual arousal was enough to bring her to her senses and make her push Silas away. She was trembling from head to foot and felt foolishly close to tears. What she was feeling made her feel both vulnerable and confused. She didn't even know how it had happened—or why.

Penny Jordan has been writing for more than twenty years and has an outstanding record: over 130 novels published, including the phenomenally successful A PERFECT FAMILY; TO LOVE, HONOUR AND BETRAY; THE PERFECT SINNER and POWER PLAY, which hit the *Sunday Times* and *New York Times* bestseller lists. Penny Jordan was born in Preston, Lancashire, and now lives in rural Cheshire.

Recent titles by the same author:

MASTER OF PLEASURE
PRINCE OF THE DESERT
THE ITALIAN DUKE'S WIFE

THE CHRISTMAS BRIDE

BY

PENNY JORDAN

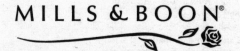

MILLS & BOON®

All the characters in this book have no existence outside the imagination of the author, and have no relation whatsoever to anyone bearing the same name or names. They are not even distantly inspired by any individual known or unknown to the author, and all the incidents are pure invention.

First published in Great Britain 2006
Harlequin Mills & Boon Limited,
Eton House, 18-24 Paradise Road, Richmond, Surrey TW9 1SR

© Penny Jordan 2006

ISBN-13: 978 0 263 84864 9
ISBN-10:   0 263 84864 7

Set in Times Roman 10½ on 12¾ pt
01-1206-46873

Printed and bound in Spain
by Litografia Rosés, S.A., Barcelona

THE
CHRISTMAS BRIDE

PROLOGUE

'IT'S A total nightmare, it just couldn't be any worse.'

'Spending Christmas in a castle in Spain is a nightmare?'

Tilly gave a reluctant smile as she heard the wry note in her friend and flatmate's voice.

'Okay. On the face of it, it may sound good,' she agreed. 'But, Sally, the reality is that it will be a nightmare. Or rather a series of on-going nightmares,' she pronounced darkly.

'Such as?'

Tilly shook her head ruefully. 'You want a list? Fine! One, my mother is about to get married to a man she's so crazily in love with she's sends me e-mails that sound as though she's living on adrenalin and sex. Two, the man she's marrying is a multimillionaire— no, a billionaire—'

'You have a funny idea of what constitutes a nightmare,' Sally interrupted.

'I haven't finished yet,' Tilly said. 'Art—that's ma's billionaire—is American, and has very strong ideas about Family Life.'

'Meaning?'

'Patience. I *am* getting there. Ma's got this guilt thing that it's her fault that I'm anti-men and marriage, because she and Dad split up.'

'And is it?'

'Well, let's just say the fact that she's been married and divorced four times already doesn't exactly incline me to look upon marriage with optimism.'

'Four times?'

'Ma loves falling in love. And getting engaged. And getting married. This time Ma has decided she wants to be married at the stroke of midnight on New Year's Eve in a Spanish castle. So Art is transporting his entire family to spend Christmas and New Year in Spain to witness the ceremony—at his expense. We're all going to stay at the castle so that we can get to know one another properly "as a family". Because, according to Ma, Art can't think of a more Family Time than Christmas.'

'Sounds good so far.'

'Well, here's the bit that is not so good. Art's family comprises his super-perfect daughters from his first marriage, along with their husbands and their offspring.'

'And?'

'And Ma, for reasons best known to herself, has told Art that I'm engaged to be married. And of course Art has insisted that I join the happy family party at the castle, along with my fiancé.'

'But you haven't got a fiancé. You haven't even got a boyfriend.'

'Exactly. I have pointed this out to my mother, but she's pulling out all the high-drama stops. She says she's afraid Art's daughters are going to persuade him not to marry her, and that if I turn up *sans* fiancé it will add fuel to their argument that as a family we are not cut out for long-term, reliable marriages. She should really have gone on the stage.' Tilly looked at her friend. 'I know this sounds crazy, but the truth is I'm worried about her. If Art's daughters are against the marriage, then she won't stand a chance. Ma isn't a schemer. She just can't help falling in love.'

'It sounds more like you're the parent and she's the child.'

'Well, Ma does like to imply that she was little more than a child when she ran off with my father and had me. Although she was twenty-one at the time, and the reason she ran off with Dad was that she was already engaged to someone else. Who she then married after she realised she had made a mistake in marrying my dad.' Tilly was smiling as she spoke, but there was a weary resignation in her tone. 'I feel I should be there for her, but I just don't want her to blame me if things go wrong because I didn't turn up with a fiancé.'

'Well, you know what to do, don't you?'

'What?'

'Hire an escort.'

'*What?*'

'There's no need to look like that. I'm not talking about a "when would you like the massage" type escort. I'm talking about the genuine no-strings, no-sex, perfectly respectable and socially acceptable paid-for social escort.'

Sally could see that Tilly was looking both curious

and wary. 'Come on, pass me the telephone directory. Let's sort it out now.'

'You could always lend me Charlie,' Tilly suggested.

'Let you take my fiancé away to some Spanish castle for the most emotionally loaded holiday of the year for loved-up couples?' Sally gave a vehement shake of her head. 'No way! I'm not letting him miss the seasonal avalanche of advertisements for happy couples with their noses pressed up against jewellers' windows.' Sally balanced the telephone book on her lap. 'Okay, let's try this one first. Pass me the phone.'

'Sally, I don't…'

'Trust me. This is the perfect answer. You're doing this for your mother, remember!'

'Will I do *what*?' Silas Stanway stared at his young half-brother in disbelief.

'Well, I can't do it. Not in a wheelchair, with my arm and leg in plaster,' Joe pointed out. 'And it seems mean to let the poor girl down,' he added virtuously, before admitting, 'I need the money I'll be paid for this, Silas, and it's giving me some terrific contacts.'

'Working as a male escort?' Beneath the light tone of mockery Silas felt both shock and distaste. Another indication of the cultural gap that existed between him, a man of thirty plus, and his barely twenty-one-year-old sibling—the result of his father's second marriage—for whom Silas felt a mixture of brotherly love and, since their father's death, almost paternal concern.

'Loads of actors do it,' Joe defended himself. 'And this agency is *respectable*. It's not one of those where the women you escort are going to come on to you for sex. Mind you, from what I've heard they're willing to pay very well if you do, and it can be a real turn-on in a sort of Mrs Robinson way. At least that's what I've heard,' he amended hastily, when he saw the way his half-brother was looking at him. 'It's only for a few days,' he wheedled. 'Look, here's the invite. Private jet out to Spain, luxury living in a castle, and all at the expense of the bridegroom. I was really looking forward to it. Come on, be a sport.'

Silas looked uninterestedly at the invitation Joe had handed to him, and then frowned when he saw the name of the bridegroom-to-be. 'This is an invitation to Art Johnson the oil tycoon's wedding?' he demanded flatly.

'Yeah, that's right,' Joe said with exaggerated patience. 'Art Johnson the Third. The girl I'm escorting is the daughter of the woman he's going to marry.'

Silas's eyes narrowed. 'Why does she need an escort?'

'Dunno.' Joe gave a dismissive shrug. 'She probably just hasn't got a boyfriend and doesn't want to show up at the wedding looking like a loser. It's a woman thing; happens all the time,' Joe informed him airily. 'Apparently she rang the agency and told them she wanted someone young, hunky and sexy, Oh, and not gay.'

'And that doesn't tell you *anything?*' Silas asked witheringly.

'Yeah, it tells me she wants the kind of escort she can show off.'

'Have you met her?'

'No. I did e-mail her to suggest we meet up beforehand to set up some kind of background story, but she said she was too busy. She said we could discuss everything during the flight. The bridegroom is organising the private jet. All I have to do is get in a taxi, with my suitcase and passport, and collect her from her place on the way to the airport. Easy-peasy. Or at least it would have been if this hadn't happened during that rugby match.' Joe grimaced at his plaster casts.

Silas listened to his half-brother's disclosures with growing contempt for the woman who was 'hiring' him. The more he heard, the less inclined he was to believe Joe's naive assertion that his escort duties were to be strictly non-sexual. Ordinarily he would not only have given Joe a pithy definition of exactly what he thought of the woman, he would also have added a warning not to do any more agency work and a flat refusal to step into his brother's shoes.

Normally. If the bridegroom in question had not been Art Johnson. He had been trying to contact Art Johnson for the last six months for inside information about the late legendary oil tycoon Jay Byerly. Jay Byerly had, during his lifetime, straddled both the oil industry and the political scene like a colossus.

As an investigative journalist for one of the country's most prestigious broadsheets, Silas was used to interviewees being reluctant to talk to him. But this time he was investigating for a book he was writing about the sometimes slippery relationships within the oil industry. And Jay Byerly was rumoured to have once used his connections to hush up an oil-related near-ecological disaster nearly thirty years ago. Until recently Art

Johnson had been a prime mover in oil, and he had been mentored by Jay Byerly in his early days.

So far every attempt Silas had made to get anywhere near Art Johnson had been met with a complete rebuff. Supposedly semi-retired from the oil business now, having handed over the company to be run by his sons-in-law, it was widely accepted that Art still controlled the business—and its political connections—from behind the scenes.

Silas wasn't the kind of man who liked being forced to give up on anything, but he had begun to think that this time he had no choice.

Now it seemed fate had stepped in on his side.

'Okay,' he told his half-brother. 'I'll do it.'

'Wow, Silas—'

'On one condition.'

'Okay, I'll split the fee with you. And if she does turn out to be a complete dog—'

'That condition being that you don't do any more escorting.'

'Hey, Silas, come on. The money's good,' Joe protested, but then he saw Silas's expression and shook his head. 'Okay... I guess I can always go back to bar work.'

'Right. Run through the arrangements with me again.'

CHAPTER ONE

THERE was no way this was going to work. No way she was ever going to be able to persuade anyone that a hired escort was her partner for real, Tilly decided grimly. But why should she care? Given free choice, she wouldn't even be going to the wedding. Her mother hadn't picked a decent partner yet, and Tilly had no faith in her having done so this time. And as for Art's family… Tilly tried to picture her fun-loving, rule-breaking, shock-inducing mother living happily within the kind of family set-up she had described to Tilly in her e-mails, and failed.

The marriage would not last five minutes. In fact it would, in Tilly's opinion, be better if it never took place at all—even if her mother was adamant that she was finally truly in love.

She was a fool for letting herself be dragged into her mother's life to act the part of the happily engaged daughter. But, as always where anything involving her mother was concerned, it was always easier to give in than to object.

The only thing Tilly had ever been able to hold out

about against her mother was her own determination never to fall in love or marry.

'But, darling, how can you say that?' her mother had protested when Tilly had told her of her resolve. 'Everyone wants to meet someone and fall in love with them. It's basic human instinct.'

'What if I find out that I'm not in love with them any more, or they aren't in love with me?'

'Well, then you find someone else.'

'Only to marry again, and then again when that doesn't work out? No, thanks, Ma.'

Mother and daughter they might be, and they might even share the same physical characteristics, but sisters under the skin they were most definitely not.

No? Who was she kidding? Wasn't it true that deep down she longed to meet her soul mate, to find that special someone to whom she'd feel able to give herself completely, with whom she'd feel able to remove all those barriers she had erected to protect herself from the pain of loving the wrong man? A man strong enough to believe in their love and to demolish all her own doubts, noble enough to command not just her love but her respect, human enough to show her his own vulnerability—oh, and of course he must be sexy, gorgeous, and have the right kind of sense of humour. The kind of man that came by the dozen and could be found almost anywhere then, really, she derided herself. Just as well she had never been foolish enough to tell anyone about him. What would she say? *Oh, and by the way, here's a description of my wish for Christmas...*

Get a grip, she warned herself sternly. He—her

'fiancé', and most definitely *not* soul mate—would be here any minute. Tilly frowned. She had e-mailed him last night to explain in exact detail what his role would involve, and to say that he would be required to pose convincingly as her fiancé in public. And only in public. No matter how many times Sally had assured her that she had nothing to worry about, and that hiring an escort was a perfectly reasonable and respectable thing to do, Tilly was not totally convinced.

Luckily, because she hadn't taken any time off during the summer, getting a month's leave from her job now had not been a problem. However, she could just imagine what the reaction of the young and sometimes impossibly louche male trainee bankers who worked under her would be if they knew what she was doing.

Other women in her situation might think of themselves as being let loose in a sweet shop at having so many testosterone-charged young men around. Tilly, however, tended to end up mothering her trainees more than anything else.

She tensed when she heard the doorbell ring, even though she had been waiting for it. It was too late now to wish she had taken Sally up on her offer to go into work later, so that she could vet the escort agency's choice.

The doorbell was still ringing. Stepping over her suitcase, Tilly went to open the door, tugging it inwards with what she had intended to be one smooth, I'm-the-one-in-control-here movement.

But her intention was sabotaged by the avalanche of female, hormone-driven reactions that paralysed her, causing her to grip hold of the half-open door.

The man in front of her wasn't just good-looking, she recognised with a small gulp of shock. He was… He was… She had to close her eyes and count to ten before she dared to open them again. Tiny feathery flicks of sensual heat were whipping against her nerve-endings, driving her body into a fever of what could only be lust. This man didn't just possess outstanding male good looks, he also possessed that hard-edged look of dangerous male sexuality that every woman recognised the minute she saw it. Tilly couldn't stop looking at him. He was dark-haired and tall—over six feet, she guessed— with powerfully broad shoulders and ice-blue eyes fringed with jet-black lashes. And right now he was looking at her with a kind of frowning impatience, edged with cool, male confidence, that said he certainly wasn't as awestruck by her appearance as she was by his.

'Matilda Aspinall?' he asked curtly.

'No…I mean, yes—only everyone calls me Tilly.' For heaven's sake, she sounded like a gauche teenager, not an almost thirty-year-old woman capable of running her own department in one of the most male-dominated City environments there was.

'Silas Stanway,' he introduced himself.

'*Silas?*' Tilly repeated uncertainly. 'But in your e-mails I thought—'

'I use my middle name for my e-mail correspondence,' Silas informed her coolly. It wasn't entirely untrue. He *did* use his middle name, along with his mother's maiden name as his pen-name. 'We'd better get a move on. The taxi driver wasn't too keen on stopping on double yellows. Is that your case?'

'Yes. But I can manage it myself,' Tilly told him.

Ignoring her attempts to do exactly that, he reached past her and hefted the case out of the narrow hallway as easily as though it weighed next to nothing.

'Got everything else?' he asked. 'Passport, travel documentation, keys, money…'

Tilly could feel an unfamiliar burn starting to heat her face. An equally unfamiliar sensation had invaded her body. A mixture of confusion and startlingly intense physical desire combined with disbelieving shock. Why was she not experiencing irritation that he should take charge? Why was she experiencing this unbelievably weird and alien sense of being tempted to mirror her own mother's behaviour and come over all helpless?

Was it because it was Christmas, that well-known emotional trap, baited and all ready to spring and humiliate any woman unfortunate enough to have to celebrate it without a loving partner? Christmas, according to the modern mythology of the great god of advertising, meant happy families seated around log fires in impossibly large and over-decorated drawing rooms. Or, for those who had not yet reached that stage, at the very least the loved-up coupledom of freezing cold play snow fights, interrupted by red-hot passionate kisses, the woman's hand on the man's arm revealing the icy glitter of a diamond engagement ring.

But, no matter how gaudily materialism wrapped up Christmas, the real reason people invested so much in it, both financially and emotionally, was surely because at heart, within everyone, there was still that child waking up on Christmas morning, hoping to receive the most perfect present—which the adult world surely translated as the gift of love, unquestioning, unstinting, freely given and equally freely received. A gift shared and celebrated, tinsel-wrapped in hope, with a momentary suspension of the harsh reality of the destruction that could follow.

She knew all about that, of course. So why, *why*, deep down inside was she being foolish enough to yearn to wake up on her own Christmas morning to that impossibly perfect gift? *She* was the one who was in charge, Tilly tried to remind herself firmly. Not him. And if he had really been her fiancé there was no way she would have allowed him to behave in such a high-handed manner, not even bothering to kiss her…

Kiss her?

Tilly stood in the hall and stared wildly at him, while her heart did the tango inside her chest.

'Is something wrong?'

Those ice-blue eyes didn't miss much, Tilly decided. 'No, everything's fine.' She flashed him her best "I'm the boss" professional smile and stepped through the door.

'Keys?' This woman didn't need an escort, she needed a carer, Silas decided grimly as he watched Tilly hunt feverishly through her bag for her keys and then struggle to insert them into the lock. It was just as well that Joe *wasn't* the one accompanying her. The pair of them wouldn't have got as far as Heathrow without one of them realising they had forgotten something.

What was puzzling him, though, was why on earth she had felt it necessary to hire a man. With those looks and that figure he would have expected her to be fighting men off, not paying them to escort her. Normally his own taste ran to tall, slim soignée brunettes of the French persuasion—that was to say women of intelligence who played the game of woman-to-man relationships like grand chess masters. But his hormones, lacking the discretion of his brain, were suddenly putting up a good argument for five foot six, gold and honey streaked hair, greenish-gold eyes, full soft pink lips, and a deliciously curvy hourglass figure.

He had, Silas decided, done Joe more than one favour in standing in for him. His impressionable sibling wouldn't have stood a chance of treating this as a professional exercise. Not, of course, that Silas was tempted. And even if he had been there was too much at stake from his own professional point of view for him to risk getting physically involved with Matilda. Matilda! Who on earth had been responsible for giving such a beauty the name Matilda?

What was the matter with her? Tilly wondered feverishly. She was twenty-eight years old, mature, responsible, sensible, and she just did not behave like this around men, or react to them as she did to this man. It wasn't the man who was causing her uncharacteristic behaviour, she reassured herself. It was the situation. Uncomfortably she remembered that sharp, hot, sweetly erotic surge of desire she had felt earlier. Her body still ached a little with it, and that ache intensified every time her female radar picked up the invisible forcefield of male pheromones surrounding Silas. Her body seemed to be reacting to them like metal to a magnet.

She grimaced as she looked up at the December

grey-clouded sky. It had started to rain and the pavement was wet. Wet, and treacherously slippery if you happened to be wearing new shoes with leather soles, Tilly recognised as she suddenly started to lose her balance.

Silas caught her just before she cannoned into the open taxi door. Tilly could feel the strength of his grip through the soft fabric of the sleeve of her coat and the jumper she was wearing beneath it. She could also feel its warmth…*his* warmth, she recognised, and suddenly found it hard to breathe normally. Who would have thought that such a subtle scent of cologne—so subtle, in fact, that she had to stop herself from leaning closer so she could smell it better—could make her feel this dizzy?

She looked up at Silas, intending to thank him for saving her from a fall. He was looking back down at her. Tilly blinked and felt her gaze slip helplessly down the chiselled perfection of his straight nose to his mouth. Her own, she discovered, had gone uncomfortably dry. So dry that she was tempted to run the tip of her tongue along her lips.

'I 'aven't got all day, mate…'

The impatient voice of the taxi driver brought Tilly back to reality. Thanking Silas, she clambered into the taxi while he held the door open for her before joining her.

Joe would never have been able to deal with a woman like this, Silas decided grimly as the taxi set off. Hell, after the way she had just been looking at his mouth, he was struggling with the kind of physical reaction that hadn't caught him so off-guard since he had left his teens behind. In the welcome shadowy interior of the cab he moved discreetly, to allow his suit jacket to conceal the tell-tale tightness of the fabric of his chinos.

'Why don't I take charge of the passports and travel documentation?' he suggested to Tilly. 'After all, if I'm supposed to be your escort—'

'My fiancé,' Tilly corrected him.

'Your *what*?'

'You did get my e-mail, didn't you?' she asked uncertainly. 'The one I sent you explaining the situation, and the role you would be required to play?'

For the first time Silas noticed that she was wearing a solitaire diamond ring on the third finger of her left hand.

'My understanding was that I was simply to be your escort,' he told her coolly. 'If that's changed…'

There was a look in his eyes that Tilly wasn't sure she liked. A cynical world-weary look that held neither respect nor liking for her. What exactly was a man like this doing working for an escort agency anyway? she wondered. He looked as though he ought to be running a company, or…or climbing mountains—not hiring himself out to escort women.

'You will be my escort, but you will also be my fiancé. That is the whole purpose of us going to Spain.'

'Really? I understood the purpose was for us to attend a wedding.'

She hadn't mistaken that cynicism, Tilly realised. 'We *will* be attending a wedding. My mother's. Unfortunately my mother has told her husband-to-be that I am engaged—don't ask me why; I'm not sure I know the answer myself. All I do know is that, according to her, it's imperative that I turn up with a fiancé.'

'I see.' And he did. Only too well. He had been right to suspect that there was a seedy side to this whole escort situation. His mouth compressed and, seeing it, Tilly began to wish that the agency had sent her someone else. She didn't think she was up to coping with a man like this as her fake fiancé.

'What else was in this e-mail that I ought to know about?'

Tilly's chin lifted. 'Nothing. My mother, of course, knows the truth, and naturally I've told her that we will have to have separate rooms.'

'Naturally?' Silas quirked an eyebrow. 'Surely there is nothing *natural* about an engaged couple sleeping apart?'

Tilly suspected there would certainly be no sleeping apart from a woman he was really involved with. Immediately, intimate images she hadn't known she was capable of creating filled her head, causing her to look out of the taxi's window just in case Silas saw in her eyes exactly what she was thinking.

'What we do in private is our business,' she told him quickly.

'I should hope so,' he agreed, *sotto voce*. 'Personally, I've never seen the appeal of voyeurism.'

Tilly's head turned almost of its own accord, the colour sweeping up over her throat with betraying heat.

'Which terminal do you want, gov?' the taxi driver asked.

'We're flying out in a privately owned plane. Here's where we need to go.' Tilly fumbled for the documents, almost dropping them when Silas reached out and took them from her, his fingers touching hers. She was behaving like a complete idiot, she chided herself, as Silas leaned forward to give the taxi driver directions—and, what was more, behaving like an idiot who was completely out of her depth.

Probably because she *felt* completely out of her depth. Silas just wasn't what she had been expecting. For a start she had assumed he would be younger, more like the boys at work than a man quite obviously in his thirties, and then there was his raw sexuality. She just wasn't used to that kind of thing. It was almost a physical presence in the cab with them.

How on earth was she going to get through nearly four weeks of pretending that he was her fiancé? How on earth was she going to be able to convince anyone, and especially Art's daughters, that they were a couple when they were sleeping in separate rooms? This just wasn't a man who *did* separate rooms, and no woman worthy of the name would want to sleep apart from him if they were really lovers. Anxiously she clung to her mother's warning that her husband-to-be was very moralistic. They could say that they were occupying separate rooms out of respect for his views, couldn't they?

'We're here,' Silas said as the taxi jerked to a halt. 'You can explain to me exactly what is going on once we're on board.'

She could explain to him?

But there was no point arguing as he had already turned away to speak with the taxi driver.

CHAPTER TWO

THE only other occasion when Tilly had travelled in a private jet had been in the company of half a dozen of her male colleagues, and the plane had been owned by one of bank's wealthiest clients. She hadn't dreamed then that the next time she would be driven up to the gangway of such a jet, where a steward and stewardess were waiting to relieve them of their luggage and usher them up into luxurious comfort, the jet would be owned by her stepfather-to-be.

Tilly wasn't quite sure why she found it necessary to draw attention to her large and fake solitaire "engagement ring" by playing with it when she saw the way the stewardess was smiling at Silas. It certainly seemed to focus both the other girl's and Silas's attention on her, though.

'Ms Aspinall.' The male steward's voice was as soothing as his look was flattering. 'No need to ask if you travel a lot.' He signalled to someone to take their luggage on board. 'Everyone in the know travels light and buys on arrival—especially when they're flying to somewhere like Madrid.'

Tilly hoped her answering smile didn't look as

false as it felt. The reason she was 'travelling light', as he had put it, was quite simply because she had assumed that this castle her mother's new man had hired came complete with a washing machine. The demands of her working life meant that she rarely shopped. A couple of times a year she restocked her working wardrobe with more Armani suits and plain white shirts.

But, bullied by Sally, she had allowed herself to be dragged down Knightsbridge to Harvey Nicks, in order to find a less businesslike outfit for the wedding, and a dress for Christmas day. The jeans she was wearing today were her standard weekend wear, even if they were slightly less well fitting than usual, thanks to her anxiety over her mother's decision to marry again.

Once inside the jet she settled herself in her seat, trying not to give in to her increasing urge to look at her new 'fiancé,' who seemed very much at home in the world of the super-rich for someone who needed to boost his income by hiring himself out as an escort.

Jason, the steward, offered them champagne. Tilly didn't drink very much, but she accepted the glass he was holding out to her, hoping that it might help ease the tension caused by her unwanted awareness of Silas's potent sexuality. Silas, on the other hand, shook his head.

'I prefer not to drink alcohol when I'm flying,' he told Jason. 'I'll have some water instead.'

Why did she suddenly feel that drinking one glass of champagne had turned her into a potential alcoholic who couldn't pass up on the chance to have a drink? Rebelliously she took a quick gulp of the fizzing bubbles, and then tried not to pull a face when she realised how dry the champagne was.

They were taxiing down the runway already, the jet lifting easily and smoothly into the grey sky. Tilly wasn't a keen flyer, and she could feel her stomach tensing with nervous energy as she waited for the plane to level off. Silas, on the other hand, looked coolly unmoved as he reached for a copy of the *Economist*.

'Right, you'd better tell me what's going on,' he said, flicking through the pages of the magazine. 'I was informed that you wanted an escort to accompany you to your mother's wedding.'

'Yes, that's right—I do,' Tilly agreed. 'An escort who is my fiancé—I did explain it all to you in the e-mail I sent,' she insisted defensively when she saw the way he was looking at her.

'E-mails are notoriously unreliable.' But not, perhaps, as unreliable at passing on information as his dear brother, Silas acknowledged grimly. 'You'd better explain again.'

Tilly glanced over her shoulder to make sure they were alone in the cabin. This was her mother's new man's plane, staffed by his employees. 'My mother's husband-to-be is an American. He has very strong ideas about family life and…and family relationships. He has two daughters from his first marriage, both married with children, and my mother…' She paused and took a deep breath. Why on earth should she be finding this so discomfiting? As though somehow she were on trial and had to prove herself? She was the one hiring Silas, the one in charge, not the other way around.

'My mother feels that Art's daughters aren't entirely happy about their marriage.'

Silas's eyebrows lifted. 'Why not? You've just said that they're both married with children. Surely they should be happy to see their father find happiness?'

'Well, yes... But the thing is...'

Tilly chewed anxiously on her bottom lip—a small action which automatically drew Silas's attention to her mouth. How adept the female sex was at focusing male attention on it, Silas thought cynically. Mind you, with a mouth as full and soft-looking as hers, Tilly hardly needed to employ such tired old tricks to get a man to look at it and wonder how it would feel beneath his own. His imagination had been there already, and gone further. Much further, in fact, he admitted reluctantly.

How did she put this, Tilly wondered, without being disloyal to her mother? 'My mother doesn't think that Art's daughters feel she will make him happy.'

'Why not?'

'Well, he's a widower, and Ma is a divorcee.'

Silas gave a small brusque shrug. 'So your mother made a mistake? It's hardly unusual in this day and age.'

'No...but...'

'But?'

'But Ma has made rather more than just one mistake,' Tilly informed him cautiously.

'You mean she's been married more than once?'

'Yes.'

'How much more than once?'

'Well, four times, actually. She can't help it.' Tilly defended her mother quickly when she saw Silas's expression. 'She just falls in love so easily, you see, and men fall in love with her, and then—'

'And then she divorces them, and starts over with a bigger bank balance and a richer man?'

Tilly was shocked. 'No! She's not like that. Ma would never marry just for money.'

Silas registered the 'just' and said cynically, 'But she finds it easier to love a rich man than one who is poor?'

'You're just like Art's daughters and their husbands. You're criticising my mother without knowing her. She loves Art. Or at least she believes she does. I know it sounds illogical, but Ma *is* illogical at times. She's afraid that Art's daughters will be even more antagonistic towards her if they know that I'm single. Art was boasting to her about his daughters and their marriages, and Ma lost the plot a bit and told him that I was engaged.'

It was such a ridiculous story that it had to be true, Silas decided. 'And you don't know any single available men you could have asked to help you out?'

Of course she did. She knew any number of them. But none whom she felt she could rely on to act the part convincingly enough.

'No, not really.' How easily the fib slipped from her lips. She was obviously more her mother's daughter than she had known, she admitted guiltily. But Silas knew nothing of her personal and professional circumstances—or the fact that she would have rather walked barefoot over hot coals than let the boisterous and youthful sexual predators who made up her staff know about her lack of a sexual partner. Even if it was by choice. As far as Tilly was concerned it was a small and harmless deceit—she wasn't to know that Silas, in between flying in and out of the country to complete an assignment in Brussels after his meeting with Joe, had done as much background-checking on her as he could, and thus knew exactly what her professional circumstances were.

No available men in her life? Silas was hard put to it to bite back the cynical retort he longed to make and ask why she didn't use her status as the head of her own department to provide herself with a fake fiancé from one of the ten-plus young men who worked under her.

On the other hand, for reasons he was not prepared to investigate too closely, it brought him a certain sense of relief to know that he had found her out as a liar and therefore not to be trusted. And he certainly wasn't going to be taken in by that pseudo-concern she had expressed for a mother who sounded as though she was more than a match for any number of protective daughters and their husbands.

Not, of course, that Art's daughters were exactly your run-of-the-mill average daughters. Silas had learned all about them when he had done his initial search on their father. They had learned their politics and their financial know-how at their father's knee, and while they adopted a Southern Belle manner in public, in private they were not just steel magnolias but steel magnolias with chariot spikes attached to their wheels.

More than one person had been eager to relate to him some of the urban mythology surrounding the family, about the way Art's daughters had targeted their husbands-to-be: disposing of a couple of fiancés, and at least one illegitimate child, plus a handful of quashed drink-driving and drug charges on their way to the altar.

If one thing was certain it was that they would not tolerate their father marrying a woman they themselves had not sourced and checked out.

'Okay, so your mother is afraid that her potential step-daughters might persuade their father not to go ahead with the wedding. But I still don't understand how you turning up with a fiancé can have any effect on that.'

'Neither can I, really, but my mother was getting herself in such a state it just seemed easier to give in and go along with what she wanted.'

'Easier, but surely not entirely advisable? I should have thought a calm, analytical discussion—'

'You don't know my mother. She doesn't *do* calm or analytical,' Tilly said, before adding protectively, 'I'm making her sound like a drama queen, but she isn't. She's just a person who lives in and on her emotions. My guess is that she simply got carried away with trying to compete with Art in the perfect daughter stakes. I've told her that I've managed to find someone to pose as my supposed fiancé, but I haven't told her about using the agency,' she warned. 'She'll probably assume that I already knew you.'

'Or that we're past lovers?'

Tilly was aghast. She shook her heed vehemently. 'No, she won't think that. She knows that I—'

'That you what? Took a vow of chastity?'

For some reason the drawling cynicism in his voice hurt. 'She knows that I don't have any intention of ever getting married.'

'Because you don't believe in marriage?'

Tilly gave him a level look and replied coolly, 'No, because I don't believe in divorce.'

'Interesting.'

'Not really. I daresay any number of children with divorced parents feel the same way. Why are you asking me so many questions? You sound more like a…a barrister than an actor. I thought actors liked talking about themselves, not asking questions.'

'I can assure you that I am most definitely *not* a barrister. And surely actors need to study others in order to play their roles effectively?'

Not a barrister. But she was astute enough to have recognised his instinctive need to probe and cross-question, Silas recognised.

What was it about the quality of a certain kind of silence that made a person feel so acutely uncomfortable? Tilly wondered as she hunted feverishly for a safer topic of conversation. Or in this instance was it the man himself who was making her feel so acutely conscious of things about herself and her attitude to life? Things she didn't really want to think about.

'I was a bit worried that the agency wouldn't be able to find someone suitable who was prepared to work over Christmas,' she offered, holding out a conversational olive branch as brightly as she could in an attempt to establish the proper kind of employer—her—and employee—him—relations. Not that it was true, of course. The truth was that she would have been delighted if Sally's plan to provide her with a fiancé had proved impossible to carry through.

'If that's a supposedly subtle attempt to find out if I have a partner, the answer is no, I don't. And as for working over Christmas, any number of people do it.'

Tilly had to swallow the hot ball of outrage that had lodged in her throat. She could almost visualise the small smouldering pile of charcoal that had been her olive branch.

'I was not asking if you had a partner. I was simply trying to make polite conversation,' she told him.

'More champers?'

Tilly smiled up at Jason in relief, welcoming his interruption of a conversation that was leading deeper and deeper into far too personal and dangerous territory. Far too personal and dangerous for *her*, that was.

'We'll be landing in ten minutes,' Jason warned them. 'There'll be a car and driver waiting for you, of course.'

Tilly smiled, but less warmly.

'What's wrong?' Silas asked her.

'Nothing. Well, not really.' She gave a small shrug as Jason moved out of earshot. 'I know I should be enjoying this luxury, and of course in a way I am, but it still makes me feel guilty when I think about how many people there are struggling just to feed themselves.'

'A banker who wants to save the world?' Silas mocked her.

Immediately Tilly tensed. 'How did you know that? About me being a banker?'

Silently Silas cursed himself for his small slip. 'I don't know. The agency must have told me, I suppose,' he said dismissively.

'Sometimes it's easier to change things from the

inside than from the outside,' Tilly explained after a slight pause.

'Indeed. But something tells me that it would take one hell of a lot of inner change to get the City types to think about saving the planet. Or were you thinking of some kind of inducement to help them? A new Porsche, perhaps?'

'Toys for boys goes with the territory, but they grow out of them—usually about the same time as their first child is born,' Tilly told him lightly.

The jet had started its descent, and Jason's return to the cabin brought their conversation to an end.

CHAPTER THREE

Snow in Spain. Who knew? She supposed *she* ought to have done, Tilly admitted, as she huddled deeper into her coat, grateful for the warmth inside the large four-wheel drive that had been waiting at the airport to transport them up to the castle.

Silas had fired some rapid words in Spanish to their driver at the start of their journey, but had made no attempt to engage her in conversation, and the long, muscular arm he had stretched out across the back of the seat they were sharing was hardly likely to give anyone the impression that they were besotted with one another.

The castle was up in the mountains, beyond the ancient town of Segovia. Tilly had viewed the e-mail attachment her mother had sent, showing a perfect fairy-tale castle against a backdrop of crisp white snow, but foolishly she hadn't taken on board that the snow as well as the castle was a reality. Now, with the afternoon light fading, the landscape outside the car windows looked more hostile than beautiful.

It didn't help when Silas suddenly drawled, 'I hope you've packed your thermals.'

'No, I haven't,' she was forced to reply. 'But the castle is bound to be centrally heated.'

The now-familiar lift of dark eyebrows made her stomach lurch with anxiety.

'You think so?'

'I know so. My mother hates the cold, and she would never tolerate staying anywhere that wasn't properly heated.'

'Well, she's *your* mother, but my experience is that most owners of ancient castles hate spending money on heating them—especially when they are hiring them out to other people. Maybe on this occasion, since your mother, like us, has love to keep her warm, she won't feel the cold.'

Tilly gave him a look of smouldering antipathy. 'That wasn't funny.'

'It wasn't meant to be. Have you given any real thought as to just how intimately we'll have to interact with each other, given that we're going to be part of a very small and potentially very explosive private house party?'

'We won't have to interact intimately at all,' Tilly protested, hot-faced. 'People will accept that we're an engaged couple because we'll have told them we are. We won't be expected to indulge in public displays of physical passion to prove that we're engaged. Besides, I'm wearing a ring.'

She was totally unprepared for the sudden movement he made, reaching for her hand and taking possession of it. His fingers gripped her wrist, his thumb placed flat against her pulse so that it was impossible for her to hide the frantic way it was jumping and racing.

'What are you doing?' she demanded crossly, when he removed her fake ring with one deft movement.

'You don't really imagine that *this* is going to deceive the daughters of a billionaire, do you?' he taunted, shaking his head as he put it in his pocket. 'They'll know straight away it's a fake, and it's only a small step from knowing your ring is a fake to guessing our relationship is fake.'

Tilly couldn't conceal her dismay. His confidence had overpowered her own belief in the effectiveness of her small ploy.

'But I've *got* to wear a ring,' she told him. 'We're supposed to be engaged, and it's as her properly engaged daughter that my mother wants to parade me in front of Art and his daughters.'

'Try this.'

Tilly couldn't believe her eyes when Silas reached into his jacket pocket and removed a small shabby jeweller's box.

Uncertainly she took it from him. He couldn't possibly have *bought* a ring.

'Here, give it to me.' he told her impatiently, after he'd watched her struggle with the catch, and flicked it open so easily that she felt a complete fool. Warily she looked at the ring inside the box, her eyes widening in awe. The gold band might be slightly worn, but the rectangular emerald surrounded by perfect, glittering white diamonds was obviously very expensive and very real.

'Where—? How—?' she began.

'It was my mother's,' Silas answered laconically.

Immediately Tilly closed the box and tried to hand it back to him.

'What's wrong?'

'I can't wear your mother's ring.'

'Why not? It's certainly a hell of a lot more convincing than that piece of cheap tat you were wearing.'

'But it's your *mother's*.'

'It's a family ring, not her engagement ring. She didn't leave it to me with strict instructions to place it only on the finger of *the* woman, if that's what you're thinking. She wasn't sentimental, and I daresay she had stopped believing in Cinderella and her slipper a long time before she died.'

'Do you always carry it round with you?' Tilly asked him. Her question was uncertain, and delivered in an emotional whisper.

Silas looked at her. He couldn't remember the last time he had met a woman who was as absurdly sentimental as this one appeared to be. Silas didn't *do* sentimentality. He considered it to be a cloying, unpleasant emotion that no person of sound judgement should ever indulge in.

'Hardly,' he told her crisply. 'It just happens that I recently had it revalued for insurance purposes, and I collected it from the jewellers on my way over to you. I was on my way to the bank to put it in my safety deposit box, but the traffic was horrendous and we couldn't miss the flight. If one were to assess the odds, I should imagine it will be safer on your finger that it would be in my pocket.'

He sounded as though he was telling the truth, and he certainly did not look the sentimental type, Tilly acknowledged.

'Give me your hand again.' He took hold of it as he spoke, re-opening the box and obviously intending to slide the ring onto her finger. Immediately she tried to stop him, shaking her head.

'No, you mustn't do that,' she said. A small icy finger of presentiment touched her spine, making her shiver. She could see the mix of derision and impatience in the look he was giving her, and although inwardly she felt humiliated by his obvious contempt, she still stood her ground.

'What's wrong now? Worried that you're breaking some fearful taboo or something?' he demanded sarcastically.

'I don't like the idea of you putting the ring on. It seems wrong, somehow,' Tilly admitted.

'Oh, I see. My putting my ring on your engagement finger when we aren't engaged is wrong, but pretending that we are engaged when we aren't is perfectly all right?'

'It's the symbolism of it,' Tilly tried to explain. 'There's something about a man putting a ring on a woman's finger... It might sound illogical to you—'

'It does, and it is.' Silas stopped her impatiently, taking hold of her hand again and slipping the ring onto her finger.

Tilly had told herself that it couldn't possibly fit, but extraordinarily it did—and perfectly. So perfectly that it might have been made for her—or meant for her? What on earth had put that kind of foolish thought into her head?

'There, it's done. And nothing dramatic has happened.'

Not to him, maybe, Tilly acknowledged, but something *had* happened to her. The worn gold felt soft and heavy on her finger, and inside her chest her heart felt as constricted as though the ring had been slipped around it. When she looked down at her hand the diamonds flashed fire. Or was it the tears gathering in her own eyes that were responsible for the myriad rainbow display of colours she could see?

This wasn't how a ring like this should be given and worn, and yet somehow just by wearing it she felt as though she had committed to something. Some message, some instinctive female awareness the ring was communicating to her. A sense of pain and foreboding filled her, but it was too late now. Silas's ring was on her finger, and they were coming into Segovia, the lights from the town illuminating the interior of the car.

'What was she like?' Tilly asked softly, the question instinctive and unstoppable.

'Who?'

'Your mother.'

Silas wasn't going to answer her, but somehow he heard himself saying quietly and truthfully, 'She was a conservationist, wise and loving, and full of life. She died when I was eight. She was in a protest. Some violence broke out and my mother fell and hit her head. She died almost immediately.'

Tilly could feel the weight of the silence that followed his almost dispassionate words. Almost dispassionate, but not quite. She had sensed, even if she had not actually heard, the emotion behind them. She looked down at the ring and touched it gently, in tribute to the woman to whom it had belonged.

Silas had no idea why he had told Tilly about his mother. He rarely thought about her death these days.

He was very fond of his stepmother, who had shown him understanding and kindness, and who had always respected his relationship with his father, and he certainly loved Joe. Damn all over-emotional, sentimental women. A wise man kept them out of his life, and didn't make the mistake of getting involved with them in any way. There was only one reason he was here with Tilly now, and that was quite simply because she was providing him with the opportunity to get close to Art. And if that meant that he was using her, then he wasn't going to feel guilty about that. She, after all, was equally guilty of using him.

'I hadn't expected the castle to be quite so remote,' Tilly admitted, nearly half an hour after they had driven through Segovia, with its picturesque buildings draped in pretty Christmas decorations. 'Nor that it would be so high up in the mountains.'

They had already passed through the ski centres of Valdesqui and Navacerrada, looking as festive as a Christmas card, and although the snow-covered scenery outside the car was stunningly beautiful in the clearness of the early-evening moonlight, Tilly was surprised that her mother, who loved sunshine and heat, had chosen such a cold place for her wedding.

They turned off the main road onto a narrow track that wound up the steep mountainside, past fir trees thick with snow, towards the white-dusted, fairy-tale castle perched at its summit, lights shining welcomingly from its many tall, narrow windows. The castle was cleverly floodlit, heightening the impression that it had come straight out of a fairy story, and the surrounding snow was bathed in an almost iridescent pale pink glow

'It's beautiful,' Tilly murmured appreciatively. Silas glanced at her, about to tell her cynically that it looked like something dreamed up by a Hollywood studio. But then he saw the way the moonlight filling the car illuminated her face, dusting her skin with silvery light and betraying her quickened breathing.

Extraordinarily and unbelievably his mind switched track, and suddenly he was asking himself if he held her under him and kissed her, with a man's fierce need for a woman's body, would that pulse in her throat jump and burn the way the pulse in her wrist had done when he had held her hand? And would that pulse then run like a cord to the stiffening peak of her breast when he circled the place where the smooth pale flesh gave way to the soft pink aureole? Would that too swell in erotic response to his touch, a moan of pleasure suppressed deep in her throat causing her pulse to jump higher, while he rolled her nipple between his thumb and forefinger, savouring each further intimacy, knowing what her small restless movement meant? Knowing, too, that she would be wet and hungry for him—

Abruptly Silas blocked off his thoughts. It startled him to discover just how far and how fast they had travelled on their own erotic journey without his permission. He wasn't given to fantasising about sex with a woman he was in a relationship with, never mind one who was virtually a complete stranger to him. He didn't need to fantasise about sex, since it was always on offer to him should he want it. But, just as he was revolted by the thought of eating junk food, so, equally, he was turned off by the idea of indulging in junk sex. Which was probably why he was feeling like this now, with an erection so hard and swollen that it actually felt painful. He had been so busy working these last few months that he hadn't had time to get involved in a relationship. The ex with whom he occasionally had mutually enjoyable release sex had decided to get married, and he couldn't really remember the last time he had spent so much time in close proximity to a woman in a non-sexual way. And *that*, no doubt, was why his body was reacting like a hormone junkie who had the promise of a massive fix.

Their driver turned the four-wheel drive into the inner courtyard of the castle, coming to a stop outside the impressive iron-studded wooden doors.

Tilly smiled at the driver as he held open her door for her and helped her out. The courtyard had been cleared of snow, but she could still smell it on the early-evening air, and there was a shine on the courtyard floor that warned her the stones underfoot would be icy.

The huge double doors had been flung open, and Tilly goggled to see two fully liveried footmen stepping outside. Liveried footmen! She was so taken aback she forgot to watch where she was walking, and gasped with shock as she stepped onto a patch of ice and started to lose her balance.

Hard, sure hands gripped her arms, dragging her back against the safety of an equally hard male body.

And there she stood, her back pressed tightly into Silas's body, his arms wrapped securely around her, as her mother and the man Tilly presumed must be her

mother's new fiancé stood in the open doorway,
watching them. Her reaction was instinctive and disas-
trous. She turned her head to look at Silas, intending to
demand that he release her, but when she realised how
close she was to his mouth all she could do was look at
it instead, while the hot pulse of lust inside her became
a positive volcano of female desire. She lifted her
hand—surely not because she had actually intended to
touch him, to trace the outline of that firmly shaped
male mouth with its sensually full bottom lip? Surely
she had not actually intended to do that? No, of course
not. She simply wasn't that kind of woman. How could
she be when she had spent the better part of her young
adult life training herself not to be? All she had wanted
to do was to push her hair back off her face. And that
was what she would have done too, if Silas hadn't
caught hold of her hand.

The hand on which she was wearing his mother's
ring. A hard knot of emotions filled her chest cavity and
blocked her throat. An overwhelming sense of sadness
and love and hope.

'Silas…' Her lips framed his name and her eyes filled
with soft warm tears.

What the hell was a going on? Silas wondered in disbelief. One minute he was reacting instinctively to save
an idiotic female from falling over; the next he was
holding her in his arms and getting an emotional
message he couldn't block, feeling as if he was experiencing something of such importance that it could be the
pivot on which the whole of his future life would turn.

He watched as Tilly's lips framed his name, and felt

the aching drag of his own sexual need to bend his head to hers and to explore the shape and texture of her mouth. Not just once, but over and over again, until it was imprinted on his senses for ever. So that he could recall its memory within a heartbeat. So that he could hold it to him for always.

Silas tensed as he heard the sharp ring of an inner warning bell.

This was not a direction in which he wanted to go. This kind of emotional intensity, this kind of emotional dependency, was not for him. And certainly not with a woman like this. Tilly had lied to him once already. He did not for one moment believe the sob story of concerned and loving daughter she had used when describing her mother's marriage history. Logic told him that there had to be some darker and far more selfish reason for what she was doing. As yet he hadn't unearthed it— but then he hadn't tried very hard, had he? After all, he had his own secret agenda. He might not have discovered her hidden motive, but that didn't mean it didn't exist. For now he was content to play along with her game, and the role she had cast for him, because it suited his own purposes. But this looking at her mouth and feeling that he'd stepped into another dimension where emotion and instinct held sway rather than hard-headed logic and knowledge had to be parcelled up and locked away somewhere.

In the few seconds it had taken for him to catalogue his uncharacteristic reaction, Tilly's face had started to glow a soft pink.

'Darling…'

Abruptly Tilly wrenched her unwilling gaze from Silas's mouth to focus on her mother.

Physically, Annabelle Lucas looked very much like her daughter, although where Tilly downplayed her femininity, Annabelle cosseted and projected hers. Slightly shorter than Tilly, she had the same hourglass figure, and the same honey and butter-coloured hair. However, where Tilly rarely wore make-up, other than a hint of eyeshadow and mascara and a slick of lipgloss, Annabelle delighted in 'prettifying' herself, as she called it. Tilly favoured understated businesslike suits, and casual clothes when she wasn't working; Annabelle dressed in floaty, feminine creations.

Tilly tried to wriggle out of Silas's grip, but instead of letting her go he bent his mouth to her ear and warned, 'We're supposed to be a deliriously loved-up, newly engaged couple, remember?'

Tilly tried to ignore the effect the warmth of his breath against her ear was having on her.

'We don't have to put on an act for my mother,' she protested. But she knew her argument was as weak as her trembling knees.

The arch look her mother gave them as she hurried over to them in a cloud of her favourite perfume made Tilly want to grit her teeth, but there was nothing she could say or do—not with her mother's new fiancé within earshot.

'Art, come and say hello to my wonderful daughter, Tilly, and her gorgeous fiancé.'

Her mother was kissing Silas with rather too much enthusiasm, Tilly decided sourly.

'How sweet, Tilly, that you can't bear to let go of him.'

Tilly heard her mother laughing. Red-faced, she tried to snatch her hand back from Silas's arm, but for some reason he covered it with his own, refusing to let her go.

'Silas Stanway,' Silas introduced himself, extending his hand to Art, but still, Tilly noticed dizzily, managing to keep her tucked up against him. She could have used more force to pull away, but slipping on the ice and ending up on her bottom was hardly the best way to make a good impression in front of her stepfather-to-be, she decided.

Her mother really must have been wearing rose-tinted glosses when she had fallen in love with Art, Tilly acknowledged, relieved to have her hand shaken rather than having to submit to a kiss. Fittingly for such a fairy-tale-looking castle, he did actually look remarkably toad-like, with his square build and jowly face. Even his unblinking stare had something unnervingly toadish about it.

He was obviously a man of few words, and, perhaps because of this, her mother seemed to have gone in to verbal overdrive, behaving like an over-animated actress, clapping her hands, widening her eyes and exclaiming theatrically, 'This is all so perfect! My darling Art is like a magician, making everything so wonderful for me—and all the more wonderful now that you're here, Tilly.' Tears filled her eyes, somehow managing not to spill over and spoil her make-up. 'I'm just so very happy. I've always wanted to be part of a big happy family. Do you remember, darling, how you used to tell me that all you wanted for Christmas was a big sister? So sweet. And now here I am, getting not just the most perfect husband but two gorgeous new daughters and their adorable children.'

If only her father were here to witness this, and to share this moment of almost black humour with her, Tilly thought wryly, as she wondered how her mother had managed to mentally banish the various sets of step-families she had collected via her previous marriages.

Her mother beamed, and turned away to lead them back into the house. Silas bent his head and demanded, 'What was that look for?'

Too disconcerted to prevaricate, Tilly whispered grimly, 'Ma already has enough darling ex-steps and their offspring to fill her side of any church you could name.'

'Somehow I don't think that Art would want to know that.'

'You don't like him, do you?' Tilly said, with a shrewd guess of her own.

'Do you?'

'Hurry up, you two. You'll have plenty of time for whispering to each other later, and it's cold with the door open.'

The first thing Tilly saw as she stepped into the hallway was an enormous Christmas tree, its dark green foliage a perfect foil for the artistically hung Christmas tree decorations in shades of pale green, pink and blue, to tone with the hallway's painted panelling. Suddenly Tilly was six years old again, standing between her parents and gazing up with eyes filled with shining wonder at the Christmas tree in Harrods toy department.

That had been before she had understood that when her father complained about her mother's spending habits, and the circle of friends from which he was excluded, he wasn't 'just teasing'. And that the 'uncle' her mother had been so desperate for her to like was destined to replace her father in her mother's life. That Christmas she had been so totally, innocently happy, unaware that within a year she would know that happiness was as fragile and as easily broken as the pretty glass baubles she had gazed at with such delight.

Christmas—season of love and goodwill and more marital break-ups than any other time of year. A sensible woman would take to her heels at her first sighting of a Christmas tree and not come back until the bleakness of January had brought everyone to their senses.

'What time is dinner, Ma?' Tilly asked her mother prosaically, determined to set the tone of her enforced visit from the start. 'Only, I could do with going up to my room and getting changed first.'

Behind Art's back Annabelle made a small moue, and then said in an over-bright voice. 'Oh, I am sorry, darling, but we won't be having a formal dinner. Art doesn't like eating late, and then of course we have to consider the children. The girls are such devoted mothers, they wouldn't dream of breaking their routines. Art is quite right. It makes more sense for us to eat in our own rooms. So much more comfortable than dressing up and sitting down for a five-course dinner in the dining room.'

Tilly, who knew how much her mother adored dressing up for dinner, even when she was eating alone at home, opened her mouth to ask what was going on and then closed it again.

Her heart started to sink. She knew that she wasn't

imagining the desperation she could hear in her mother's voice.

'Isn't this the most gorgeous, magical place you have ever seen?' Annabelle was saying in an artificially bright voice, as she indicated the huge octagonal hall, decorated in its sugared almond colours, from which a delicate, intricately carved marble staircase seemed to float upwards.

'It is beautiful, Ma,' Tilly agreed. 'But rather cold.'

Immediately her mother gave small pout. 'Darling, don't be such a spoilsport. There is heating, but… With the children being used to living in a controlled-temperature environment they really do need to have the benefit of what heating there is in *their* suites, even if that means that some of the other rooms have to go without.' Annabelle was heading for the stairs. 'I've put you and Silas in the same room, just like you asked me to do.'

So he had been right, Silas decided grimly. So much for this just being an innocent, escort-duties-only commission! However, before he could say anything, Art had begun to study him, frowning.

'You look familiar… Have we met somewhere before?'

Silas felt his stomach muscles clench. 'Not so far as I know,' he responded truthfully. Art had turned down all his attempts to get an interview with him, but that didn't mean Art hadn't seen his photograph somewhere, or perhaps requested information about him. And if he had…

'So what exactly is it you do?' Art persisted.

'Silas is an actor,' Tilly answered firmly for him, preempting the criticism she sensed was coming by adding determinedly, 'And a very good one.' She gave her mother a look which she hoped she would correctly interpret as *I need to talk to you urgently about this bedroom situation*, but to her dismay her mother was refusing to make eye contact. In fact, now that she looked at her mother more closely, Tilly could see how tense and on edge she was beneath her too-bright smile, how desperate she was for everyone's approval of the castle. And of herself? Was it because of this insecurity within her mother that she had always kept the gates to her own emotions firmly padlocked? Because she was afraid of becoming like her mother?

As had happened so many times in the past when she sensed that her mother was unhappy, Tilly felt her protective instinct kick in. Leaving Silas's side, she moved over to Annabelle, linking her arm with her mother's in a gesture of daughter-to-mother solidarity.

'An actor. How exciting!' Annabelle exclaimed. 'That's probably why you think Silas's face is familiar, Artie, you must have seen him in something.'

'I doubt it. It don't waste my time watching people play at make-believe.' Art gave a snort of derision.

How could her mother be in love with a man like this? Tilly wondered despairingly. Her original misgivings about the marriage were growing by the second.

She gave her mother's arm a small squeeze. 'Why don't you take me upstairs and show me the room?' she suggested lightly, adding, 'I'm sure that Silas and Art can entertain one another while we indulge in some mother-and-daughter gossip.' She knew she was taking a risk, throwing Art and Silas together without being there herself to make sure Silas didn't say the wrong thing, but right now her need to ensure they had separate rooms took precedence over everything else. 'I haven't even seen your dress yet,' she reminded her mother.

'Oh, darling, it's so beautiful,' Annabelle enthused, the tension immediately leaving her face to be replaced by a glow of excitement. 'It's Vera Wang. You know, she does all the celebrity wedding gowns. Her people swore at first that she couldn't fit me in, but Art persuaded them to relent. It's just such a pity that I didn't think to get you to come to New York at the same time, so that we could have looked for something for you. Art's grandchildren are going to be our attendants, of course. We've agreed that they'll be wearing Southern Belles and Beaux outfits, so…sweet. And it would be lovely if your Silas would give me away…'

Suddenly Tilly wanted to cry—very badly. Here was her mother, trying desperately to put a brave face on the fact that while Art had his daughters and grandchildren to provide him with family support and fill the traditional wedding roles, Annabelle had to rely on her daughter and a man who was being paid to escort her.

Swallowing hard, Tilly sniffed back the tears that were threatening to fall.

'Dad would probably have given you away if you'd asked him.'

Immediately her mother looked anxiously at Art. 'I did think of your father,' she admitted. 'But Art's daughters can't see how it's possible to maintain a platonic relationship with an ex-husband, and Art feels…well, he thinks… Well, Art agrees with them.'

The retort Tilly was longing to make had to be smothered in her throat when she saw her mother's *please don't* look.

What the hell had he got himself into? Silas wondered angrily as he watched the two women walk up the stairs arm-in-arm. Whatever was going on, mother and daughter were both in on it—and deep in it too, right up to their pretty little necks. He was being used, and not just for the escort duties he was being paid for. Annabelle had let the cat out of the bag with regard to Tilly's sexual expectations. No woman asked to share a room with a man unless she expected sex to be on the agenda. Tilly had lied to him when she had claimed they would be having separate rooms, and if it wasn't for the fact that he needed information from Art he would be calling a cab right now, to take him straight back down to the airport in Madrid. Because he didn't want to have sex with a woman he had just spent the last few hours acknowledging had a mind-blowingly intense erotic effect on his body.

Who was he kidding? Okay, so he *did* want to have sex with her—but on his terms, not hers. And he certainly wasn't going to let her get away with lying to him—even if she *had* surprised him with her determination to show Art she wasn't going to let him put Silas down for being an actor. That *had* surprised him, Silas admitted. The last woman to protect him from someone's unflattering opinion had been his mother, and he had been all of five.

Tilly was gutsy; he had to give her that. But that didn't mean he was going to let her get away with manoeuvring him into her bed. There was no real danger to him in being plunged into this kind of situation. He could handle it. But what if it had been Joe she had tricked into sharing her bed? The young idiot was green enough to have had sex with her without any thought for the possible consequences: to his health, to the fate of any child that might be conceived, to anything other than giving in to a young heterosexual male's natural reaction to being in bed with a sexually attractive woman who had invited him there.

Whereas he, of course, wouldn't be facing any of those problems? Okay, he would be facing one of them, since he wasn't in the habit of travelling everywhere with a packet of condoms. Would Tilly have thought to deal with that kind of necessity? She was certainly old enough and no doubt experienced enough to be as aware of the risks as he was himself, he decided cynically as he turned to follow his uncommunicative host into the bar.

CHAPTER FOUR

'HERE is your room, darling. It's lovely, isn't it…?'

Annabelle had thrown open the door into a room on the second floor of the castle.

More because she wanted to make sure they weren't overheard than because she was genuinely interested in her accommodation, Tilly stepped past her and into the room.

It was large, certainly. Large, and cold, and very obviously an attic room, decorated in faded cabbage rose wallpaper, and scented with the unmistakable odour of damp.

'It's got its own bathroom. With the most fabbie real Edwardian bath.'

The determined brightness in her mother's voice made Tilly's spirits plummet. Annabelle looked so vulnerable, getting angry with her felt like being unkind to a child.

Very gently Tilly took hold of her mother's hands and led her across to the large double bed, pulling her down until they were both seated on it, facing one another.

'Ma, what is going on?' she asked, as calmly as she could. 'You know that Silas and I aren't really engaged. We don't even know each other. He's just someone I've hired to pretend to be my fiancé. You *know* that. We were supposed to have separate rooms. I've *told* him that we are having separate rooms. You *assured* me that we would be having separate rooms. So what's gone wrong?'

Tears filled her mother's eyes. 'Oh, Tilly darling, please don't be cross with me. It isn't my fault. I *had* planned to put you and Silas—he is gorgeous, by the way, and he would be just perfect for you—in the most heavenly pair of interconnecting rooms. More like a suite, really, both with their own bathrooms and the most divine little sitting room, but then Art's daughters arrived and everything went horribly wrong.'

Tilly waited while her mother paused to blow her nose and clear her throat. 'You see, I hadn't realised that Susan-Jane and Cissie-Rose would want to have their children sleeping on the same floor with them, or that they would expect to have connecting rooms. But of course once Susan-Jane had explained that she and Cissie-Rose need to be close by, and how it made much more sense for them to have the suite I'd earmarked for you and Silas...

'She said that the children's nannies, and the personal assistants to Dwight and Bill—that's their husbands, of course—would also have to be on the same floor, because Dwight and Bill frequently work late at night. They have to be in touch with Head Office at all times, and having to come all this way has caused them so much disruption. I felt so guilty about that—especially when Cissie-Rose told me that the children had been upset because they wouldn't be spending Christmas at home. I don't know how it happened, but somehow or other it turned out so that they practically took up the whole of the first floor, apart from the suite Art and I are sharing, and that meant the only rooms left were up here on the second floor.'

Inwardly Tilly counted to ten. Something was telling her that her relationship with her new stepsisters-to-be was not going to be one made in heaven, she thought grimly.

'Okay, but there must be more than one room up here, Ma. I mean, there's only one bed in here—'

'Darling, I know, and I am truly sorry. But I'm sure that Silas will behave like a perfect gentleman. I mean, a man like him doesn't need to go around persuading women to have sex with him, does he? Do you know what I think?' she said brightly. 'I think that he'll probably be glad of the opportunity to be with a woman who isn't coming on to him.'

'Ma, let's stick to the point. How many rooms are there on this floor?'

'Oodles,' Annabelle told her promptly. 'But there's been a problem with the roof, apparently, and most of them are damp, and the ones that aren't are already occupied by the staff. Strictly speaking we aren't supposed to be using any of the rooms up here, according to the contract the Count's legal people gave us, but when I spoke to the *major-domo* and explained the problem he was really sweet about it, and everyone has worked so hard to get this room ready for you. I'd hate for them to think that we aren't grateful.'

Tilly wrapped her arms around her cold body. 'Ma, it's freezing in here.'

'Yes. I'm sorry about that. The Count's PA did explain to us how the heating system worked, and that we weren't to turn up any of the radiators because if we did it would mean that some others wouldn't work. And I did try to explain this to Art's daughters, but I can see their point about the children needing to be kept warm.'

Tilly could hear a strange noise in her ears. It took her several seconds to realise that it was the sound of her teeth grinding in suppressed frustration.

'Ma—'

'Please don't be difficult about this, darling. I so want everything to go well, and for all of you to get on. Art's daughters have been so sweet—offering to help me once Art and I are married, explaining to me how their social circle works. They've even warned me that some of Art's late wife's friends will be hostile to me, and that some of the men might behave towards me in a flirtatious way because of the way that I look, and because I've been married before. It's kind of them, really.'

'Is it? It sounds more to me as though they're trying to undermine you,' Tilly told her mother shrewdly, and then wished that she hadn't been so blunt when she saw the hurt look on her mother's face.

'Darling, don't say that. You're going to love them, I know. Now, why don't I leave you to unpack, while I go down to the kitchen and organise evening meals for everyone?'

'Some hot water bottles might be a good idea as well,' Tilly suggested dryly.

After her mother had gone she examined the room and its adjoining bathroom. The bath was, as her mother had said, truly Edwardian. Of massive proportions, it stood in the middle of a linoleum-covered floor in a room that was so cold Tilly was shivering even though she was still wearing her coat. There was also a shower, and a separate lavatory.

She heard the outer door reopening, and hurried back into the bedroom, saying despairingly, 'Ma. I don't— Oh, it's you.' She came to an abrupt halt as she saw Silas standing just inside the door, holding it open for a young man carrying their luggage.

She had to wait for him to put it down and leave before she could speak. 'I'm really sorry about this. My mother seems to have allowed Art's daughters to bully her into letting them take the two-bedroom suite she had earmarked for us, and this appears to be the only room that's left.'

'And presumably the only bed?' Silas asked silkily.

'I don't like this any more than you do,' Tilly assured him. 'But there's nothing I can do except offer to sleep on the floor.'

'And of course you're fully prepared to do that?'

'Actually, yes, I am,' Tilly said. She didn't like the tone he was using, and she didn't like the way he was looking at her either. If she had thought the bedroom and the icy-cold bathroom were cold enough to chill her blood, they were nothing compared to the coldness of the look Silas was giving her.

'Do you make a habit of this?' It infuriated Silas that she didn't seem to think he had the intelligence to see through what she was doing.

'Do I make a habit of what?' Tilly demanded, perplexed.

'Hiring men to have sex with you.'

Tilly was glad she had the bed behind her to sink down onto. His accusation hadn't just shocked her, it had also blocked her chest with a huge lump of indigestible and unwanted emotional vulnerability—and pain. *Pain?* Because a man she didn't know was misjudging her? Why should that cause her to feel like this? She had only just met Silas. He meant nothing whatsoever to her, and yet here she was reacting to his unpleasant remarks with the kind of hurt feelings and sense of betrayal that were more appropriate for a long-standing and far more intimate relationship. Was that it? Did she secretly *want* to have sex with him? Had he somehow sensed that, even though she hadn't been aware of it herself? Was *that* the reason for his accusation, and her own emotional reaction to it?

This time when Tilly shivered it wasn't just because she was cold. She didn't like what was happening. She had never wanted to do any of this in the first place—not coming here, not hiring herself an escort, and most certainly not sharing a bed with Silas. She took a deep breath.

'I do not hire men to have sex with me. I don't need to.' Well, it was true, wasn't it? 'I've already made it perfectly clear to you why I need an escort, and if you thought I was lying or had some ulterior motive then surely it was up to you to refuse the commission. You don't strike me as the kind of man who would allow himself to be put in a situation you don't want,' she told him shrewdly.

Her reaction wasn't what Silas had been expecting. He had assumed that she would use his accusation as an excuse to lay her cards on the table. At which point he had intended to make it plain that, while he was prepared to act as her fiancé in public, making use of the intimacy provided by their shared accommodation was most definitely not on the agenda.

The nature of his profession meant that Silas was immediately and instinctively suspicious of everyone's motives. As far as he was concerned, everyone had something to hide, something they were prepared to sell, and something they were prepared to buy. He himself wanted to hide the fact that he was using his position as a fake fiancé to get closer to Art, but he was only prepared to sell his time, not his body. He was also a man who hated being wrong-footed and forced to accept that he had made an error of judgement—especially by a woman he had no reason whatsoever to respect.

'I thought your explanation owed more to imagination than truth,' he told her uncompromisingly. 'As far as I am concerned, and in view of what has transpired, I was right to question the validity of what you were telling me. Not, I must say, that I admire your taste in sexual boltholes,' he added disparagingly. 'Apart from anything else, it's freezing. Are those radiators on?' He walked over to one of them and put his hand against it.

'Apparently Art's daughters have messed up the delicate balance of radiator temperature and fair heating for all,' Tilly told him tiredly. 'Or at least I think that's what my mother was trying to tell me.'

Somehow Tilly managed to answer his mundane question with an equally mundane answer, even though her heart was pumping so much blood through her veins she could actually feel the adrenaline surge. There was no way she was going to let his insults go unchallenged.

'You don't have to stay here, you know,' she told him. 'There's nothing to stop you leaving if you want. I certainly won't be trying.' She tried to put as much withering scorn into her words as she could.

Silas gave her a derisory look. 'We've only just arrived, and we're supposed to be engaged. I can hardly walk out now.'

'Why not?' Tilly demanded, in a brittle voice that betrayed her tension. 'Engaged couples do quarrel and break up. It happens all the time. In fact, I think it's a very good idea.'

She could feel the comfort of her own relief at the thought of him leaving. He was having an effect on her she really did not like or want. It—*he*—had made her feel uncomfortable and on edge even before he had accused her of lying to him. There was no way she wanted to spend a week sharing a room with a man who thought she was gagging for sex with him and about to pounce on him at any minute. She might be being a tad old-fashioned, but the truth was that she much preferred the traditional scenario in which *she* was the one imagining that he might pounce on *her*. Not that she wanted him to do so, of course. Not for one minute.

'In fact,' she continued fiercely, 'I think it would be an excellent idea if I went down right now to find my mother and tell her that the engagement is off.'

'Wouldn't that be somewhat counter-productive? I thought the whole idea of this was to help your mother.' The conversation and Tilly's behaviour were taking a direction Silas hadn't expected, and one he did not want. Tilly was quite obviously working herself up into a mood of moral outrage and, worse, she was throwing out the kind of challenges he had no intention of taking up.

It wasn't like him to misjudge a situation, and it irked him that he might have here. But Tilly was behaving in a way he considered out of character for the slot he had mentally fitted her into. He despised women who insisted on playing games, and normally he wouldn't have tolerated an assumed 'injured innocent' act, but right now he had too much at stake to risk her carrying out her threat. Much as he disliked having to admit it, he recognised that it night have been wiser for him to have played along with her pretence for a bit longer before letting her know that he had guessed what she was planning. He couldn't allow this new situation to accelerate.

He might not mind walking out on Tilly, but if he did he would also be walking out on his chance to talk to Art. He had already sown the seeds for what he hoped would become more informative confidences once Art had let down his guard a bit more.

He walked over to the bed and eyed it assessingly. At least it was large enough for him to ensure that Tilly kept her distance from him.

He was standing next to her when they both heard Annabelle calling out from the other side of the door. 'It's only us, darlings!'

'That's my mother now,' Tilly told him unnecessarily. 'I've made up my mind. There's no way I want to continue with this charade now, after the accusations you've just made. I'm going to tell her that we've had a row, that our engagement is over and that you're leaving.'

She was making to remove the ring he had given her as she spoke, and Silas could tell that she meant what she was saying. The door was already opening. He thought quickly, and then acted with even greater speed.

It shocked Tilly how silently and lethally fast Silas moved, dropping down onto the bed next to her and imprisoning her in his arms as he rolled her torso down under his own and then covered her mouth with his.

Tilly tried to push him away, but he was holding her too tightly, one muscular leg thrown over her in what was surely one of the most intimate embraces a fully clad couple could perform—even if he was only adopting it to keep her pinned beneath the weight of his body. Pinned in such a way that she was shockingly aware of the physical differences between them—his hardness pressed to her softness, his body dominating and unyielding, while, to her outraged horror, her own was soft and accommodating, as though her flesh welcomed the possessive maleness of his.

While she tried to grapple with her own confused reactions he started to kiss her. Not gently, but fiercely and possessively, and with an added edge of almost dangerous urgency, as though there was nothing he wanted more than to have her mouth under his, as though at any moment now he would strip the clothes from their bodies so that her only covering would be him, and then… Somehow or other his free hand was cupping her breast, the hard pad of his thumb resting against her hard nipple.

This couldn't be happening. It certainly *should* not be happening. Incredulously she struggled to resist him, distantly aware of her mother's amused, 'Whoops! Sorree…' and then the immediate closing of the bedroom door.

He could let Tilly go now. Silas knew that. The danger was over. No way could she tell her mother now that they had quarrelled and that he was leaving after what she had just witnessed. But the bedroom was bitingly cold, and the rounded warmth of Tilly's breast fitted into his hand as though it had been made for him. It surprised him to discover just how much he wanted to go on cupping it, and just how strong his urge was to caress the hard thrust of her nipple slowly and thoroughly, until she responded to his touch with her own urgency, arching up into his hands, wanting him to peel back the layers of her clothing until they could both see her arousal. He could certainly feel his own. He slid his other hand up into Tilly's hair, lifting his mouth briefly from hers, watching as her eyes opened, her gaze soft and clouded. He traced the shape of her mouth with small, teasingly light kisses that mirrored the delicate touch of his fingertips on her breast.

Tilly was hazily aware that what she was doing was very dangerous—that *Silas* was very dangerous. But the room was so cold that it seemed to be numbing her ability to respond and react in a normal way. And Silas felt so warm, lying on top of her, even if he *was* tormenting her with those tiny kisses that were compelling her to arch up to him, wanting something much more intimate. She shuddered with pleasure when he spread his fingers against her scalp and held her head while he plundered her mouth with the intimate thrust of his tongue, over and over again, until she was shuddering in the grip of the most intense physical longing she had ever experienced.

The shock of her own sexual arousal was enough to bring her to her senses and make her push Silas away. She was trembling from head to foot and felt foolishly close to tears. What she was feeling made her feel both vulnerable and confused. She didn't even know how it had happened—or why.

'You had no right to do that,' she told him, almost tearfully.

'I thought it was what you wanted.'

'*What?* How could you think that? I'd just told you that I wanted you to leave.'

Silas looked into her flushed, mutinous face and a sensation, an emotion he couldn't recognise, speared through the armour-plating of his cynicism. He lifted his hand to his chest, as though he could actually feel the sharp, unfamiliar pain as a physical reality, and then let it drop to his side as he pushed the feeling back out of the way.

'And I've just shown you that I don't want to,' he responded softly. 'In fact…right now I don't even think I want to leave this room.' A corrosive inner voice, no doubt prompted by his conscience, was demanding if not a retraction then at least an explanation of this outright lie. But he had a job to do, a truth to find, and he needed real, hard facts. As far as Silas was concerned it was his ethical duty to get those facts, and that came before any duty he might have to maintaining the same degree of truth within this current aspect of his personal life.

As ugly and unpleasant as it sounded, Tilly was using him—and he was using her. Both of them could claim that they were being forced into doing so in order to benefit others, of course. And that made it acceptable? Maybe not, but it certainly made it necessary, Silas told himself harshly.

Tilly's mouth had gone dry. She couldn't bring herself to look at him. Her heart was pounding so heavily she wanted to press her hand against her chest to calm it.

'If you're trying to imply that you…' She picked her words as carefully as she could, but they still literally stuck it her throat. 'That you want me, then I don't believe you,' she finally managed to say. 'It's less than ten minutes since you were warning me off and accusing me of hiring you for sex,' she reminded him.

'Ten minutes ago I hadn't kissed you or touched you,' Silas told her meaningfully. 'Ten minutes ago I hadn't been so turned on by the way your body was responding to my touch that right now I can't think beyond taking that response to its natural conclusion—to our mutual benefit.'

To Silas's chagrin his own words were conjuring up the most erotic images inside his head, and his body was responding powerfully to them. So powerfully that it was making it clear to him that, no matter what his brain might have to say, his body was more than willing to have sex with Tilly.

The room might still be icy cold, but suddenly Tilly

felt far too hot. He had to be lying to her, and she had better remember that. Instead of… Instead of what? Wanting him to be telling the truth? Wanting him to mean what he was saying? Wanting him to want her? Was she crazy? This kind of thing was her mother's emotional territory, not hers. She knew better. Didn't she? She started to shiver. She didn't want to stay here in this room with Silas any longer—a room that she could have sworn now smelled subtly of their mutual arousal, and his deceit, and her own foolish longing. She wanted to go back downstairs, where she would be safer—and warmer.

'It's your own fault that I kissed you, you know,' Silas told her.

Tilly had had enough. 'Look, I've already told you, I did *not* hire you to have sex with me,' she insisted fiercely.

'I didn't mean that.' Silas was smiling so tenderly at her that her insides twisted with need. 'I meant that it's your fault because when you offered me the chance to leave I knew that I couldn't, and that in turn told me how much I want you.'

Tilly stared at him. It really wasn't fair of fate to inflict this on her. It was almost Christmas, for heaven's sake, and she was very vulnerable. Silas had touched a note, a chord deep within her, that she badly wanted to ignore. It would be far too dangerous to let herself believe that he meant what he had said, and even more dangerous to admit how much she *wanted* him to have meant it.

'We've only just met,' she reminded him. 'We hardly know each other…' She was almost stuttering, she realised, as she squirmed inwardly at the sound of her own ridiculous words.

'So? Isn't fate giving us an opportunity to remedy that?' He smiled at her again, and Tilly felt her heart literally flip over inside her chest as though it were a pancake. 'She's even ensured that we'll be sharing a room, and a bed, and she's provided the added incentive of the need to share our body heat just to keep warm.'

Tilly could feel not just her face but her whole body suddenly growing hot as she curled her toes into her shoes and looked helplessly down at the bed. Things like this just did not happen to her. She wasn't that sort of person. She was too sensible, too cautious, too wary…too damn dull! She looked at Silas.

'We are engaged, after all. Who knows what might happen, or where fate might lead us?' As he spoke he reached out, sliding his fingers between her own so that they were intimately held together. 'Why don't we just let her take us where she wishes?' he suggested sexily.

'No, no, *no*! I don't want to hear any more.' Tilly put her hands over her ears in despair. 'I'm going downstairs.'

'Then I'm coming with you,' Silas said promptly. He wasn't going to give her the opportunity to end their 'engagement' in his absence.

CHAPTER FIVE

'OH, THERE you are, darlings. Oh, Tilly, you haven't even changed for dinner.' There was a reproachful note in her mother's voice that made Tilly's stomach muscles clench defensively, but she stood her ground.

'But you said it had been arranged that we'd all be eating in our rooms,' she reminded her mother, as calmly as she could.

'Oh, well, yes, I did say that. But I must have misunderstood the girls, because they've both come down dressed for dinner. Tilly, why don't you pop back up to your room and get changed into something pretty and formal? You'll have time, because the chef says that it will be another half-hour before everything will be ready.'

It was becoming increasingly plain to Tilly that Art's daughters were determined to behave as selfishly and make life as difficult for her mother as they could.

'I haven't unpacked yet, Ma,' she reminded her mother. 'And it's freezing in our room.'

'Oh, darling, please don't be such a crosspatch. What on earth will Art's girls think?'

'I daresay I might be sweeter if I had a warm bedroom,' Tilly couldn't help responding. 'And what exactly do you mean—something pretty and formal?'

'Well, the girls are both wearing the most gorgeous vintage Halston gowns. I've told them how good-looking you are, Silas, and I think they want to have a look at you,' Annabelle confided, adding blithely, 'It's dinner jackets for the men, of course—and wait until you see the drawing room and the dining room, Tilly. They are gorgeous—pure Versailles.'

Tilly had finally had enough, and she was sure that her sudden flash of temper didn't have anything to do with the thought of other women appreciating Silas's sexy masculinity. 'I don't care how gorgeous they are,' she snapped at her mother. 'I am not going back upstairs to that icebox of a room to get changed. Not, of course, that I'm not dying to show off my own vintage Oxfam.' She relented almost immediately when she saw her mother's chastened expression, going over to her to hug her tenderly, and apologising. 'I'm sorry, Ma.' How could she explain to her mother that it wasn't the cold bedroom she was dreading so much as her own desire to succumb to Silas's sexual overtures once they were in it?

'No, it's my fault, darling. I am really sorry about that dreadful room. What must Silas think of me?'

'What Silas thinks is that you've given him the perfect excuse for sharing his body warmth with his fiancée,' Silas answered promptly.

As her mother turned away Tilly shook her head at Silas and mouthed silently, *Ma knows our engagement is* fake, *remember?*

'Tilly, why don't you come to my room with me and let me find you something to borrow,' Annabelle offered.

'Yes, you go with your mother, Tee, and I'll nip up and change into my DJ,' Silas suggested.

Tee. No one had ever called her Tee before, and Tilly discovered it made her feel slightly giddy, dizzy with a dangerous sort of fizzing delight, that Silas should be the one to do so. Just as though they were really a couple, and Tee was his special pet name for her.

'You and Art have separate rooms?' Tilly queried several minutes later, as she surveyed the feminine fabric-festooned bedroom her mother was occupying.

'Art didn't think it was right that we should share, especially not with his girls and their children being here. We aren't like you modern young ones, you know, Tilly. Here, put this on. It's a bit big for me, but I think it will fit you perfectly.'

Tilly took the sliver of amber silk chiffon her mother had just removed from the wall of mirror-fronted closets and surveyed it doubtfully.

She looked at the label and then shook her head. 'Isn't this the designer who designs those outrageously sexy things that film stars' wives wear?' she asked her mother accusingly.

'Darling, it was summer when I bought it in Saint-Tropez—everyone was wearing his stuff, and I just fell in love with it. In fact, I nearly wore it the night I met Art. But then I changed my mind.'

Tilly held the dress up in front of herself and looked at her reflection in the mirror. 'This isn't a dress,' she protested. 'It's half a dozen strips of material *pretending* to be a dress.'

'Sweetheart, that's the whole secret of his style—it's all in the cut. You wait and see when you put it on. You can use my bathroom.' She was already bustling Tilly towards the opulent marble and gold-ornamented chamber that masqueraded as a bathroom. 'Oh, and why don't you put a bit more make-up on? And perhaps smooth on some of this wonderful body cream I use?'

Very determinedly, Tilly closed the door between them.

She showered first, very quickly, and then used some of the cream her mother had mentioned because her skin felt dry. It was scented, as well as gold-coloured, and she couldn't help sniffing it appreciatively as she stroked it onto her bare skin.

Now for the dress…

'Tilly? What are you doing…? Aren't you ready yet?' Annabelle knocked anxiously on the bathroom door, and when there was no response she turned the handle, relieved to discover that the door wasn't locked.

Tilly was standing in the middle of the bathroom, wearing the designer dress and staring at her reflection in the mirror.

'Oh, my!' Annabelle breathed.

'Oh, my God, don't you mean?' Tilly corrected her grimly. 'Ma, I can't possibly wear this.'

'Why not? You look gorgeous.'

'Just look at me. I'm spilling out of it everywhere. I look like a…a hooker,' Tilly said through gritted teeth.

'Sorry to interrupt you both, but Art sent me up to

find out where you are. He said to tell you that his stomach thinks his throat's been cut.

'Silas.' Annabelle beamed. 'You're just the person we need. Come and tell Tilly to stop being so silly. She looks gorgeous in this dress, but she says it makes her look like a hooker.'

Tilly's face burned as Silas stepped into view and stood studying her in silence. He had changed into a dinner suit, and her heart did its pancake trick again. How unfair it was that men should look so wonderful in their evening clothes.

'Tilly's quite right,' he announced uncompromisingly, adding softly, as her face burned with chagrin, 'and yet totally wrong. She looks like a classy, very expensive kept woman—or an equally classy and very expensive rich man's wife.' He crooked his arm. 'May I have the pleasure of escorting you both down to dinner? Because if I don't I'd better warn you that Art is going to be on his way up here, and his mood isn't good.'

Silas was smiling, but it shocked Tilly to see how apprehensive her mother suddenly looked. If they'd been on their own she would have asked her outright if she was as afraid of Art as she looked—as well as insisting that her mother loan her something else to wear. Right now, though, her concern for her mother disturbed her far more than her own self-conscious discomfort at wearing a dress that was way too revealing for her own personal taste.

Her disquiet was still with her five minutes later, when she watched Annabelle hurry over to where Art was waiting impatiently for them by the drawing room door, apologise prettily to her fiancé and reach up to kiss his cheek—or rather his jowl, Tilly thought grimly, as she tried to control her own growing unease about her mother's marriage plans.

Tilly tried to look discreetly at her watch, heaving a small sigh of relief when she saw that it was almost midnight. Tonight had to have been the worst evening of her life. How could her mother even *think* about joining a family so appallingly dysfunctional and so arrogantly oblivious to it?

Art's daughters, Susan-Jane and Cissie-Rose, were stick-thin and must, Tilly imagined, take after their mother. There was nothing of their father's heavy squareness about them. Their husbands, though, were both unpleasantly overweight. Art's daughters were, according to Tilly's mother, 'Southern Belles.' If so, they were certainly Southern Belles who had been left out in the sun so long that all humanity had been burned out of them, Tilly decided, as she listened to them deliberately and cruelly trying to destroy her mother with their innuendos and subtle put-downs.

At one point during the evening, when she had been obliged to listen politely yet again to Cissie-Rose praising herself to the skies for the high quality of her hands-on mothering, and complaining about the children's nanny daring to ask for time off over Christmas so that she could visit her own family, Tilly had longed to turn round and tell her what she thought of her. But of course she hadn't, knowing how horrified her mother would have been.

For such an apparently clean-living family, they seemed to consume an incredible amount of alcohol. Although very little food had passed what Tilly suspected were the artificially inflated and certainly perfectly glossed lips of Art's 'girls', as he referred to them. Predictably, they had expressed horror and then sympathy when Tilly had tucked into her own meal with gusto, shuddering with distaste at her appetite.

'Dwight would probably take a stick to me if I put on so much as an ounce—wouldn't you honey?' Cissie-Rose had observed.

'No guy likes an overweight gal. Ain't that the truth, Silas?' Dwight had drunkenly roped Silas into the conversation.

'Oh, you mustn't tease Silas, Dwighty,' Cissie-Rose had told her husband in her soft baby whisper of a voice. 'He and Tilly are newly engaged, and of course right now he thinks she's wonderful. I can remember how romantic it was when *we* first got engaged. Although I must say, Tilly, I was shocked when Daddy told us about the way you and Silas were carryin' on earlier.'

'T'ain't right, doing that kind of thing in a house where there's young 'uns around,' Dwight had put in.

'Which begs the point that presumably young 'un number one was sent away somewhere when young 'un number two was conceived?' Silas had murmured indiscreetly to Tilly, on the pretext of filling her wine glass.

She had desperately wanted to laugh, only too glad of the light relief his dry comment had provided, but she hadn't allowed herself. He had no business linking the two of them together in private intimate conversation of the kind only good friends or lovers exchanged.

Tilly didn't think she'd ever seen two men drink as much as Art and Dwight. Art's other son-in-law—Susan-Jane's husband, Bill, a quiet man with a warm smile, hadn't drunk as much as the other two—although Tilly suspected from the amount of attention he was paying her that either he and Susan-Jane had had a quarrel before coming down for dinner, or he was a serial flirt who didn't care how much he humiliated his wife by paying attention to another woman.

Tilly tried not to show what she was feeling when she watched Art down yet another whiskey sour, but she was relieved to see that Silas wasn't joining the other men in what seemed to be some sort of contest to see who could mix the strongest drink.

In truth, the only good thing about being downstairs was the warmth—and the excellent food. Had her room been more comfortable, and had she had it to herself, she would have escaped to it long ago, Tilly admitted as she tried and failed to smother a yawn.

'Darling, you look worn out,' Annabelle exclaimed with maternal concern. 'Art, I think we should call it a night…'

'You can call it what the hell you like, honey, but me and the boys are callin' for another jug of liquor—ain't that right, boys?'

Tilly's heart ached for her mother when she saw her anguished look.

'The staff must have had a long day, with everyone arriving. It would be considerate, perhaps, to let them clear away and get to bed?' Silas spoke quietly, but with such firm authority that everyone turned to look at him.

'Who the hell needs to be considerate to the staff? They're paid to look after us.' Dwight's face was red with resentment as he glared at Silas.

Tilly discovered that she was holding her breath, and her stomach muscles were cramped with tension. But Silas had the advantage, since he had already stood up and was moving to her chair to pull it out for her.

'You're right. I apologise if I overstepped the mark.' Silas ignored Dwight to address his apology direct to Art. 'It was only a thought.'

'And a good one Silas,' Tilly heard her mother saying heroically. 'I'm tired myself, Artie, do let's all go to bed.'

Tilly wasn't at all sure that Art would have complied if a flustered young girl hadn't come hurrying in to the room to tell Cissie-Rose that one of her children had been sick and was asking for her.

'Oh, my poor baby!' Cissie-Rose exclaimed theatrically. 'I knew coming here was gonna make her sick. I told you—you know that I did.'

'Come on. Let's make our escape now, whilst we can,' Silas muttered to Tilly.

She was tired enough to give in, going over to her mother first to give her a quick kiss, and then saying a general goodnight, while Art's daughters were still protesting in high-pitched whiny voices about the disruption to their children's routine.

'Does your mother know what she's letting herself in for?' Silas demanded as they headed for the stairs.

'I don't know,' Tilly was forced to admit. Her own

concern betrayed her into adding, 'She says she's in love with Art, but I don't see how she can be.'

By the time they reached the second floor her skin had broken out in goosebumps, and she was so cold that her longing to crawl into bed to try and get warm was overwhelming her apprehension about sharing it with Silas.

'Do you suppose there'll be any hot water up here?' she asked Silas as he opened the bedroom door for her.

'Potentially,' Silas answered her dryly. 'There's an electrically heated shower in the bathroom, although my experience of it so far suggests that it isn't totally efficient.'

'Meaning what?' Tilly asked him suspiciously.

'Meaning lukewarm is probably as good as it's going to get,' he replied. 'At least the bed should be warm, though. I went down to the kitchen earlier and borrowed a kettle and a couple of hot water bottles.'

Tilly's eyes widened, and then blurred with tired tears. Somehow he wasn't the type she had imagined doing something so domestic and so thoughtful.

He would be a fool to start feeling sorry for Tilly, Silas warned himself, hardening his heart against her obvious misery. His only purpose in being here was to get his story. And that was exactly what he intended to do, no matter what methods he had to use to do so.

'I don't think I can bear a week of this.' Tilly was too tired to care about how vulnerable her admission might make her seem. 'I hate the cold, and I hate even more the thought of not being able to have a decent hot shower whenever I want.'

Silas looked at her. 'If that's a hint that you're expecting me to be a gentleman and offer to let you use the shower first, I've got a better idea.'

'You mean I should use my mother's bathroom?' Tilly asked absently, as she stepped into the lamp-lit bedroom that looked cosier and felt slightly warmer than she had expected.

'No, I was going to say that it would make sense for us to share the shower, to make the best use of what hot water it provides.'

Was he serious? He couldn't be, could he? She looked at him, and then wished she hadn't as her body reacted to the intimacy of discovering that he was looking right back at her.

'It's warmer in here than I was expecting.' She gave him a too-bright smile to match the light tone of her voice. Anything—just as long as she didn't have to respond to the suggestion that they share a shower. Already her senses were working overtime, bombarding her with erotic messages and images.

'That's because I bribed one of the maids to find us a plug-in electric radiator.' He had closed the door and was looking at her in a way that made her heart bounce about inside her chest like a tennis ball hit by a pro. 'Now, about that shower…'

Tilly shook her head, trying to cling on to her normal, firm common sense, and to react to what he was saying as though it had been said by one of her young subordinates. The kindly but firm maternal voice of authority she used on them would surely make it plain to Silas that she wasn't expecting what he thought, as well as controlling her own dangerous longing.

'Silas, I've already told you, you've got it all wrong. You don't have to have sex with me.'

The effect of her words wasn't what she had hoped for. Instead of obediently backing off, Silas stopped leaning casually against the wall and straightened up to his full height. Such a small movement, barely more than a single step, but in terms of meaningful body language it sent her a message that had her muscles cramping with sexual tension.

'Well, that certainly isn't what my body is telling me,' he announced silkily. 'It's telling me that right now there is nothing I need or want more than to take you to bed and make love to you slowly and thoroughly and completely.'

Tilly was beyond words. She could only shake her head.

He smiled at her, and her resistance melted under the heat of the look in his eyes.

'This is crazy.' Was that quavering, somehow betraying, yearning voice really hers? 'I mean, we've only just met. We don't know one another. We're *strangers*.'

'Is there a law that says strangers can't become lovers?' He was walking very purposefully towards her now, and she felt positively light-headed with shocked excitement.

The only reason he was doing this was as a form of insurance against her threatening to break off their engagement and forcing him to leave, Silas told himself. If he could keep her happy in bed she would get what she wanted, whether she knew it or not, and he, with any luck, would get his information. The fact that he was so strongly physically attracted to Tilly wasn't what was motivating him at all. This was simply something that it was necessary for him to do.

Very necessary.

If only she was the sort of person who could just live for the moment and enjoy what that moment was offering, Tilly acknowledged giddily. If only she didn't have these crazy hang-ups about love and sex working together. If only she was able to separate them as others could. If only she didn't have even more inhibiting hang-ups about permanency and commitment, and a fear that they simply did not exist. She closed her eyes. What was wrong with her? She wanted Silas sexually so much. So why not indulge in that wanting? Why not simply offer herself up to him now? Why not slide her arms around his neck, press her body eagerly against his and lift her face for his kiss…?

Why not? Because she could not. She simply couldn't cold-bloodedly have sex with a man just because physically he turned her on. Cold-bloodedly? She was so hot for him that it hurt!

Silas was used to playing a waiting game. So why the hell did he feel so impatient now that he was tempted to cross the distance that separated them and show Tilly what they would have instead of waiting for her to agree to it?

'I'm sorry. I can't do it.' The words burst out from Tilly in a flurried tremble, causing Silas to check in mid-step and stare at Tilly in disbelief. 'It's true that I do… That is…you… Physically I *am* attracted to you,' she managed to say primly, whilst her stomach went hollow with the intensity of her body's disappointment. 'But I don't want to have sex with you.'

It surprised Silas that she was prepared to go to such lengths to show him that he had originally misjudged the situation, but what surprised him even more was how gut-wrenchingly savagely deprived he felt. The intensity of his disappointment was a measure of just how much he wanted her—and that was far too much, he decided grimly.

'If that's your decision then that's your decision,' he told her flatly. If she expected him to coax and plead she had the wrong man. Because he had no intention of doing so.

CHAPTER SIX

Tilly blinked in the darkness, luxuriating in the bed's delicious warmth. She had no idea what had woken her, unless somehow the sound of Silas's breathing had penetrated her sleep.

She was, she realised, thirsty. She remembered there was a bottle of water on the small table in front of the window. Sliding out of bed as carefully as she could so that she wouldn't disturb Silas, she made her way towards the window. Enough light was coming in through the thin curtain to guide her. She held her breath and watched Silas apprehensively, in case the sound of her uncapping the bottle woke him.

Silas was already awake, and had been awake from the second Tilly had moved and murmured in her sleep. The bed was large enough for them to sleep apart, but at some stage while she slept Tilly had moved closer to him, so that she had been sleeping almost curled into him.

As she drank her water, Tilly pulled back the curtain slightly to look out through the window, her eyes rounding with delight when she realised that it was snowing: huge, fat flakes whirling down from the moonlit sky. A childhood sense of excitement and joy she had forgotten it was possible to feel filled her, and she leaned closer to the window to watch the snow. How could something so delicate and so beautiful to watch from the safety and warmth inside also be so deadly? She was already beginning to shiver in her thin and flimsy vest, but somehow she couldn't drag herself away from the magic of watching the snow fall.

Silas studied Tilly's unguarded expression as she watched the snow. She looked as joyful and excited as a child might have done. Something that felt like a heavy stone trap door being shifted by a long-unused mechanism seemed to be happening inside his chest. Both the movement and the sensation of something touching what was raw and unprotected within him physically hurt. He badly wanted to turn over and ignore Tilly, to push back the heavy door he had locked against his own emotions. But for some reason he couldn't.

She really was cold now, Tilly admitted as she left the window to make her way carefully back to her side of the bed. The far side—which meant that she had to skirt very quietly past the end of the bed so that she didn't wake Silas.

The bed felt welcomingly warm as she slid back into it, but her feet were freezing, and as she snuggled down beneath the duvet the delicious heat coming off Silas's sleeping body acted like a magnet to her cold toes. The dip in the bed made her feel as though she was trying to go to sleep on a slope—a cold, snow-covered slope that was all the more inhospitable because of the warmth that she knew lay waiting for her if she just let her body roll a little bit closer to Silas.

She relaxed and let herself roll, luxuriating for several blissful seconds in an almost purring enjoyment of the solid wall of warm male flesh she was now lying against. Her feet seemed of their own accord to find the perfect toasty resting place on Silas's lovely warm bare calves. *Bare?* She had already been in bed when Silas had emerged from the bathroom, and of course she hadn't looked to see what he was or wasn't wearing, and she certainly wasn't going to start doing a hands-on body-check now.

Snow falling from a midnight sky, and the pleasure of exploring Silas's body with every single one of her senses divided into every individual delight they could bring. What could possibly be more perfect? She would start by looking at him, enjoying the security of the moonlit semi-darkness as she allowed her eager gaze to move over the hundreds of subtle variations of light and shadow. She would lie here doing that until it slowly got light enough to see the contours clearly.

That was if she could wait that long before she touched him. It would be a special sort of sensual heaven and hell to touch him in the darkness without previously knowing his body, to use her fingertips to guide her and to relay every nuance of his flesh, its texture firm and taut where it padded his muscles, sleek and cool over the length and strength of his bones, deliciously male-scented and erotic in the vulnerable hollows of his throat, the inside of his elbows, behind his knees.

Her own flesh seemed to be vibrating in a hymn of sensuality that was beyond her own hearing. She could feel it growing and expanding within her, deepening and tightening, filling her senses until it spilled over and flooded every bit of her.

Silas, who had been lying wide awake, gritting his teeth against his own aching desire, heard her soft moan and the accompanying acceleration of her breathing. It was too much for his self-control. He turned over, reaching for her, covering her mouth with his own before she could object and kissing her with so much skilled sensuality that she didn't even want to.

She reached up and wrapped her arms around him, trembling under the forceful pressure of her need for him as he gathered her up against himself. He *was* naked, she recognised, submitting to the starburst of heated pleasure that the knowledge brought.

When and how had she learned to open her legs just enough to be able to feel the delight of the space she had created accommodating the hard strength of his erection as he slid her down against it? His hands were sliding beneath the waist of her thin cut-offs so that he could cup her buttocks and press her more deeply against it, moving her rhythmically as he did so. Up and then down the thickness of his flesh, just a little, just enough to make her want to cry out in fierce recognition of her own aching frustration every time the movement sensitised her growing ache for a deeper intimacy.

She tried to focus away from the clamouring demands of her clitoris and to concentrate instead on the slow, explorative thrust of his tongue against her own. Only it wasn't slow any more, and she didn't know if the urgent movements galvanising her body were the result of what he was doing to her or the cause of it. She could feel the hot, tight, piercingly erotic ache of her nipples as her movements brought them into contact with his naked chest. She wanted him to touch them, to caress them, to soothe their hard need with the comfort of his kiss and then to inflame it again with the hotter, harder lash of his tongue and the rake of his teeth. She wanted him to slide her body free of her sleepwear and then explore each and every part of it while she gave herself up to the pleasure of that intimacy.

'You're going to have to provide the condom; I didn't think to bring any with me.'

Tilly stared up into Silas's face and gulped. 'Neither did I,' she told him. 'I'm a woman. They aren't the kind of thing I usually carry around with me.'

'But presumably, like me, you don't have unprotected sex?'

It was a question rather than a statement.

'I don't have sex, full stop,' Tilly admitted honestly.

She sounded so self-conscious that Silas knew immediately that she was telling the truth. He reached out and switched on the bedside lamp, keeping a firm grip on her arm when she would have squirmed away.

'It isn't that I have any problem with having sex,' Tilly assured him. 'The problem has been meeting the right kind of partner.'

Silas arched one dark eyebrow in disbelief.

'You work in the City. You're in charge of a department of testosterone-fuelled young males.'

'Exactly,' Tilly agreed vehemently, adding in exasperation when he continued to look slightly aloof and disinclined to believe her, 'Don't you see? If I started dating one of them, then it would be bound to be discussed by the others, and then they'd all…'

'Want to take you to bed?' Silas suggested, and then wished he hadn't when he was suddenly savaged by the most unexpected raw male jealousy.

'Hardly. But in order to maintain my authority over them I have to ensure that they respect me. They wouldn't do that if they thought they could have sex with me.' She gave a small shrug. 'It sounds brutal I know, but it's the truth. The City has a very macho image, and the young men working there are keen to uphold that image. They're pushing the boundaries all the time. They're like pack animals—if you show a weakness they'll sense blood and go in for the kill. If I want to date a man it has to be someone outside the City, and the hours I work make that almost impossible.'

Silas knew what she was saying was true. 'Hence your decision to include some recreational sex in the deal you set up when you hired an escort?' he suggested.

Tilly stiffened in angry outrage. 'How many times do I have to tell you that there was no such decision—either by me or for me?'

'You haven't had sex in a very long time, to judge from the way you were responding to me. It makes sense that you should think of getting a double deal for the price of one.'

Tilly's face had started to burn with the heat of her emotions. 'I *do* not and *would* not pay for sex. I've already told you that. And if that had been my intention you can be sure that I would have taken steps to ensure that I was properly protected. I don't use *any* kind of contraception,' she told him fiercely. 'Never mind carry condoms with me just in case.'

Silas could hear the emotional tears thickening her voice. If she was telling the truth then his accusations weren't just in bad taste and unfair, they were also cruel. Her need must have been very great indeed to make her respond to him as intensely as she had.

'Okay, I was out of order. You'll have to put my lack of subtlety down to the fact that I'm frustrated and disappointed as hell that we can't take this to its natural conclusion.'

Tilly gave a muffled sound and let him draw her back against his body and hold her there, with her head tucked into his shoulder.

'It's been a long time for me as well,' he told her quietly. He felt her sudden shocked movement. 'No, I'm not lying. It's the truth. Contrary to the impression I'm probably giving right now, I don't go in for impulsive spur-of-the-moment sex. My own work means that finding the right kind of partner isn't easy.'

Tilly assumed he meant that because he was an actor the opportunities were many, but so were the risks. As Sally had once graphically said to her, every time she slept with a new man she felt totally put off by the thought that she was also in part sleeping with all his previous partners—and their partners too.

'Perhaps I'm not thinking laterally enough,' Silas murmured.

'About finding a sexual partner?'

'No, about having the satisfaction of giving you the

pleasure and fulfilment I want to give you. After all, we don't need a condom to achieve that.'

Tilly's heart somersaulted, and then slammed into her chest wall. She didn't know now whether to feel shocked or excited, and ended up feeling a mix of both, tinged with wary resoluteness.

'If you're saying that because you *still* think I hired you with the ulterior motive of having sex with you—' she began.

But Silas didn't let her finish her objection, putting his fingers to her lips instead to silence her, and then bending his head to her ear to tell her meaningfully, 'Right now I ache like hell with frustration, and, like I said, it's the best way I can think of to go at least partway towards getting rid of that.'

'By satisfying *me*?'

Silas could hear the disbelief in her voice. 'I don't know what kind of men you've known, but I can't believe they haven't shown you how much pleasure a man can get from bringing his partner to fulfilment. From seeing it in her eyes, feeling it in her kiss, from witnessing that he's satisfied her.'

'There haven't been *men*,' Tilly felt obliged to admit. 'Just one man. It was when we were at university, and I felt I should…'

She'd only had *one* previous lover? Silas was caught off-guard by the wave of unexpected tenderness that surged through him. And even more startled by the ease with which he could accept the truth of what she had said.

He started to pull her down against him, his hands shaping her body, but Tilly resisted.

'What's wrong?' he asked. 'Don't you want me to?'

'Yes,' Tilly told him honestly, pausing before she said, even more honestly, in a small breathless rush of words, 'But I want our first time together to *be* together.'

It seemed a long time during which she had to bear his silent scrutiny before Silas reacted to what she had said, but when he did it wasn't with words. Instead he cupped her face, brushing the soft quiver of her lips over and over again with the pad of his thumb before bending his head to kiss her so intimately that she was afraid that she might actually orgasm after all.

When he finally lifted his mouth from hers it made her shiver in delicious awareness of his arousal to hear the thick roughness in his voice when he said, 'I wonder if you know how much I was tempted to break all my own rules on health and irresponsibility? But, while I might have broken them for myself, I don't have the right to expect you to break your own rules for me. Another time we'll have to organise things better.'

Not the most romantic words in the world, perhaps, but to Tilly they had a meaning and depth to them that went beyond the lightweight glitter of mere romance. 'What are the plans for today?' Silas asked.

'I'm not sure,' Tilly admitted. 'But if it's possible I wouldn't mind going back into that town we came through on the way here. I feel I ought to get the children a small Christmas present each.'

Silas hesitated for a second. From his own point of view it made sense for him to spend as much time as he could with Art, and yet he felt strangely reluctant to pass up on the opportunity to have Tilly to himself and get to know her better.

'I'll see if I can find out the best way for us to get into town, if you like,' he offered. After all, they were here for a week. Plenty of time for him to get close to Art later.

CHAPTER SEVEN

'DARLING. I hope you won't be offended, but I'm afraid you and Silas are going to have to entertain yourselves today, because the florist is coming out from Madrid to see me this morning, and then this afternoon I need to finalise the menu with the chef.'

'Don't worry about us, Annabelle,' Silas answered, before Tilly could say anything. 'Art, I hope you don't mind,' he continued. 'Before we joined you for break-fast I took the liberty of having a word with the chap who is in charge of your fleet of vehicles here to ask if there was any possibility of us borrowing a car and driving down into Segovia. We had to leave London in a bit of a rush and we both still have some essential Christmas shopping to do. Martin said it was okay with him if I borrowed one of the four-wheel drives so long as you had no objections.'

'Of course he doesn't—do you, sweetheart?' Annabelle smiled, looking relieved. 'You are so lucky, Tilly, to have such a thoughtful fiancé. Art hates going shopping.'

'Maybe Silas doesn't mind because *he* isn't a billionaire.'

Tilly felt a rush of anger on her mother's behalf as Art's younger daughter dropped the venom-tipped words onto the now-silent air of the room where they had eaten breakfast. It was no wonder her husband was looking embarrassed and shame-faced, Tilly decided, feeling sorry for him.

However, it was Silas who took up the gauntlet on her mother's behalf, saying coolly, 'I daresay the experience of bringing up two daughters has made Art wise enough to see through predatory females.'

The insult was delivered so lightly and easily that it was almost like a fine needle plunged into the heart, Tilly decided. You knew you'd received a mortal wound, but you couldn't see how or where. That it *had* been delivered, though, was obvious in the sudden red flush on Susan-Jane's face.

When Tilly had woken up alone in the attic bedroom that morning, she had been torn between hurrying to get showered, dressed and out of the room before Silas returned, because she felt so embarrassed about the previous night, and an equally strong impulse to remain hidden under the bedclothes, because she wasn't sure she could face Silas at all. In the event he had behaved so naturally towards her that it had been unexpectedly easy to return his good-morning kiss when he had come into the dining room several seconds behind her, smelling of cold air and explaining that he had been outside.

Now, of course, she knew why. Just as she knew what the nature of the essential shopping he had referred to was.

For a man who was perilously close to being an out-of-work actor, he possessed a rare degree of self-confidence. In fact the lack of flamboyance in his manner, allied with the cool purposefulness he displayed, seemed to Tilly to be closer to the behaviour of the top handful of her clients—wealthy, self-assured men, some of whom had inherited their wealth and some of whom had made it from scratch, but all of whom were the kind of men who didn't need to prove anything to anyone, and to whom other men seemed to automatically defer.

'I've told Martin that we should be ready to leave at about eleven,' Silas told Tilly. He glanced at his watch, which looked simple and robust but, as Tilly well knew from the boys on her team, was an expensive and highly covetable Rolex. 'That gives us just over half an hour to get ready. Is that enough time? Or shall I—?'

'Half an hour is fine,' Tilly assured him.

She was just about to push back her chair and go up to the bedroom to get her coat when Cissie-Rose suddenly announced, 'I was planning to take the kids into Segovia myself today. They're so bored, cooped up here. Since you're driving in, Silas, we may as well come with you, so that Daddy will still have the other SUV here if he needs to go out.'

'You could be spoiling Silas and Tilly's fun if you do that,' her husband chuckled.

'Oh, don't be silly. Silas won't mind. After all, it's not as if he's still courtin' Tilly. I mean, Tilly and Silas are practically living together—even though they aren't legally married yet.'

For bitchiness, Art's daughters would take some beating, Tilly decided, as Silas stood up to pull her chair out for her. She tried to imagine how she might be feeling right now if she and Silas *were* newly engaged and passionately in love, desperate for some time alone. Oddly enough it wasn't hard at all for her to conjure up exactly what she would feel. In fact it wasn't very much different from what she *was* feeling, she admitted. Which meant *what*, exactly? Because she and Silas *weren't* engaged, and they *weren't* in love. But something was happening between them, and she couldn't pretend that it wasn't. Last night, for instance... The ache last night's interrupted lovemaking had left behind, like a tamped-down fire, smouldering beneath the surface, suddenly burst into fresh life.

All the way up the stairs, too conscious of Silas, walking alongside her, Tilly struggled to smother her aching desire. It overwhelmed her that she should feel like this for a man she barely knew. Inside herself a monumental tug of war seemed to be taking place, between her head and her heart. She knew as surely as she knew her own name that she was someone who could only touch the heights of her own sensuality when her physical desire was equalled by her emotional commitment. Loveless sex had no appeal at all for her, which was why she had always held back from allowing herself to get involved with anyone. Up until now.

So what had happened to make things so different? Silas had happened, that was what! Silas, an out-of-work actor, who hired himself out as an escort. She, with all she knew about the vulnerability of love, was actually admitting that she was close to committing the insanity of falling in love with a man engaged in just about the most relationship-unfriendly career there was. She was kidding, right? She was simply testing herself—seeing how far she could stretch her self-imposed boundaries; she wasn't seriously falling in love with a man she had only just met. She couldn't be.

They had reached their bedroom door. Silas opened it for her.

'Thanks for saying what you did to Cissie-Rose. I wanted to say something myself, but I know if I had it wouldn't have been anything like such a masterly put-down.'

Silas gave a dismissive shrug. 'It was obvious when she tried to make a dig about your mother being motivated by money that that is *exactly* what motivates her. There's something profoundly ugly and depressing about the pathetic need the sons and daughters of the very wealthy often seem to have, to ring-fence their parents' assets and stick a "mine all mine" label on them.' He gave another shrug. 'Mind you, I suppose if you've been brought up to think that everything can be bought, including your own love, the thought of anyone else getting their hands on your parents' money is threatening. Makes me glad my own father was just comfortably off.'

Yes, she could see him in the social background described by the brief sketch he had just drawn. Good school, and a good university too, she judged shrewdly. The kind of background she would normally have expected to lead to a career in the City, or the law. 'Is there a tradition of acting in your family?' she asked curiously.

'Like the Redgraves, you mean?' He shook his head. 'No.'

His half-brother's desire to act had surprised them all, and it had been Silas who had had to act as a bridge between Joe and their father in Joe's early teenage years, when he had first decided he wanted to act.

'Disappointed that I'm not connected to theatre aristocracy?' he asked dryly.

It was Tilly's turn to shake her head. 'No, not at all. It's just that I find it hard to imagine you as an actor, somehow. You don't seem the type.'

'No? So what type do I seem, then?' This was dangerous territory, but he couldn't resist asking her—even as he was inwardly deriding himself for his predictable male vanity.

'Something big in the City—not a City-boy type. Something else, perhaps in one of the controlling bodies, a sort of overlooking and critical role.'

Her perspicacity reminded him that he was not dealing with a woman of Art's daughters' ilk. Tilly didn't only have far more humanity than them, she also had far more intelligence. Intelligence in a lover when you were keeping something hidden from them was not exactly an asset, he warned himself. But it was too late for him to backtrack now. Last night he had made Tilly the kind of promises—verbally as well as non-verbally—that were likely to cause him an awful lot of problems.

'Is it my imagination, or is this room actually slightly warmer?' Tilly asked.

She was glad of an excuse to change the subject and get away from the personal. Not that she didn't want to find out as much about Silas's background and his way of life as she could—she did. In fact she craved details about him. But that in itself was enough to make her want to take to her heels and put as much distance between them as she could. She was involved in a tug of war, with her head pulling in one direction and her heart in another.

'I had a word with the Count's PA,' Silas said. 'Apparently the Count won't be too pleased if he finds out his instructions with regard to the necessity of keeping all the rooms equally heated have been ignored. Even the insurance on this place is dependent on certain conditions—one of which is keeping all the rooms equally heated. I doubt that even Art, with all his billions, would be too happy if he were landed with a bill for the renovation work on one damaged castle.'

'Art's daughters aren't going to be very pleased.'

'Probably not, but they are free to take up their argument with the PA if they wish to.' He paused, and then asked dryly, 'I know it's none of my business, but does your mother have *any* idea of what she's taking on?'

'My mother prefers to only see what she wants to see, and right now what she wants to see is that Art is a wonderful man and his daughters are going to be loving stepdaughters to her. She's so unworldly. I can't help worrying about her,' Tilly admitted.

'So who does the worrying about you?'

'No one,' Tilly answered promptly. 'No one needs to worry about me. I'm not like my mother. The way she falls in love and then falls out of it again would leave me too disillusioned to keep on looking for Mr Right, but she seems to be able to pick herself up and start all over again.'

Silas could hear the underlying troubled note in Tilly's voice. It was his opinion that her mother was rather shallow, but the more he saw of Annabelle the less inclined he was to think of her as being avaricious or manipulative. 'How old were you when your mother fell out of love with your father?'

The unexpectedness of his own abrupt question startled Silas as much as it did Tilly.

'I was six when they divorced, and from what they've both told me the marriage had been in trouble for some time. I think Dad tried to stay the course because of me, but Ma had had enough.' Tilly opened the wardrobe and removed her coat and boots.

'You're going to need something a bit sturdier than those,' Silas warned her. 'Martin told me that they're expecting a fresh fall of snow later today.'

'I don't have anything else,' Tilly admitted ruefully. 'I shall have to see what I can buy while we're out. It didn't register properly with me that the weather was going to be like this.'

'If we had really come here as a newly engaged couple I daresay we'd have been only too happy to use the snow as an excuse to stay up here in bed. And no doubt we would have come prepared,' Silas said.

Tilly could feel her face turning pink, and the surge of longing that gripped her body was so intense that it made her give a small, low gasp of protest. She placed her hand flat to her lower body, in an attempt to quell the pulse of raw need that had kicked into life.

She could see from Silas's expression that he knew exactly what she was feeling. When he stepped towards her, she protested shakily, 'No.' But she didn't make any attempt to step back or to avoid him when he cupped her shoulder with one hand and slid the other into the small hollow of lower back, determinedly propelling her towards him.

'That look says you ache for me in the same way I do for you.' Even the warmth of his breath as he murmured the words against her ear was a form of caress and arousal, making her quiver with pleasure and exhale on a small, shuddering breath, desperate to turn her face to his so that his mouth would be closer to her own.

What was it about this particular woman that made him behave in ways that ran counter to all his plans? Silas wondered grimly. This agonisingly sharp and re-lentlessly demanding stab of need burning through him wasn't what he had intended at all. It had to be some-thing in the small quiver within her body that alerted him to her physical susceptibility to him that was re-sponsible for this fierce, male, *driven* urge within him, pushing him to cover her mouth with his own, rather than any independent desire of his own. It had to be. Otherwise... Otherwise, what? Otherwise he would be getting himself into a situation that he couldn't control?

'We'd better go downstairs before Martin thinks we've changed our minds and we don't want the car any more.'

She was glad that he wasn't taking things any further, Tilly told herself firmly, when Silas released her and started to step back.

'Don't do that!' Silas groaned, almost dragging her back into his arms.

'Don't do what?' Tilly protested.

'Don't look at me as though all you want is the feel of my mouth on yours,' Silas told her harshly.

'I wasn't—' Tilly began to object, but it was too late. Silas had imprisoned her face between his hands and he was bending towards her, his kiss silencing her.

Long after she should have been asleep the night before she had lain awake, desperately trying to tell herself that Silas's kisses couldn't possibly have been as wonderful as she was now thinking. She had derided herself for being bewitched by a potent combination of her own physical desire, the moonlight outside on the snow and the proximity of Christmas. She had told herself sternly that if Silas had kissed her, say, in her own flat in London, she probably wouldn't have been affected by him at all. But here she was, being swept up under last night's magical spell all over again—and if anything this time his effect on her was even more intense. If he chose to pick her up and carry her over to the waiting bed now, she knew that she wouldn't want to stop him.

An intense ache pulsed deep in the core of her sexuality. She wanted him so badly she felt shocked, almost drugged, by the overwhelming strength of her need. Panic flared inside her, causing her to push Silas away. She didn't want to feel like this about any man, and especially *his* kind of man.

The minute he released her she headed for the door. When he reached it ahead of her she held her breath, half fearful and half hopeful that he would lean against it, barring her exit, but instead he opened it for her, simply saying, 'Don't forget your coat.'

* * *

'Right, kids, you get in the back with Matilda. You won't mind if I sit in front with you, Silas, will you? Only I get so carsick if I sit in the back.'

Not a word of apology to *her*, Tilly seethed, as Cissie-Rose appropriated the passenger seat of the large four-wheel drive. Unlike her, Cissie-Rose seemed to have arrived in Spain well equipped for the snow, Tilly realised, as she looked a little enviously at her expensive winter sports-style outfit.

'I want a window seat.'

'So do I.' Cissie-Rose's children were already clambering into the back seat.

'You'll have to sit in the middle, Tilly,' Cissie-Rose instructed—for all the world as though she were some kind of servant, Tilly thought crossly.

'One of the children will have to sit in the middle. Not Tilly,' Silas intervened, in the kind of voice that said there would be no argument. 'They can take turns to have the window seat—one when we drive out and the other when we drive back.'

'*Maria* always sits in the middle,' the elder of Cissie-Rose's sons piped up.

'Maybe she does. But Tilly is not Maria.'

'Goodness, what a fuss you're making, Tilly,' Cissie-Rose said spitefully, and so blatantly untruthfully that Tilly was too taken aback to retaliate.

'Call this an SUV?' the older boy commented derogatively. 'You should see our SUVs back home.'

'Fix my seat belt for me,' the other commanded Tilly in a disagreeable voice.

She was just leaning forward to help him when Silas stopped her. *'Please will you help me with my seat belt, Tilly?* That's what I think you meant to say, isn't it?'

Tilly couldn't help feeling a bit sorry for the two boys. They were only young, and it was obvious their mother was the type of woman who treated her sons as useful bargaining tools—to be fussed over when it suited her, and then be dismissed and kept out of her way when it didn't.

For the entire length of the time it took them to drive into Segovia Cissie-Rose focused her attention on Silas—to such a degree that she and the children might just as well not have been there, Tilly decided, more upset on behalf of the children than for herself. After all, Silas had already shown her that he had no interest in Cissie-Rose, and without knowing quite how it had happened Tilly discovered that she was actually allowing herself to trust him. That would make her dangerously vulnerable, an inner voice warned her, but Tilly chose to ignore it. In fact she was choosing to ignore a lot of warnings from her inner protective voice since she had met Silas.

The boys, once they realised Tilly wasn't the kind of person who could be cowed or spoken to in the way they were used to speaking to Maria, the young girl Cissie-Rose hired to look after them, began to respect her calm firmness and even responded to it. Tilly liked children, and she enjoyed enlivening the journey for the boys, teaching them some simple travel games and talking to them about their sports and hobbies.

To Silas, forced to endure the unwanted intimacy of Cissie-Rose's deliberate and unsubtle touches to his arm and occasionally his thigh, as she underlined various points of an unutterably boring monologue, the snatches of giggles reaching him from the back seat felt like longed-for sips of clean, cold water after the cloying taste of cheap corked wine. He could only marvel at the miraculous way in which Tilly was drawing out Cissie-Rose's two young sons. Something about her calm, matter-of-fact way of talking to them touched a chord in his own memory. Inside his head he could almost hear the echo of his own mother's voice, and with it his own responding laughter.

No child should have to grow up without a mother. He had been lucky in his stepmother, he knew that, and he genuinely loved her, but listening to Tilly had brought to life an old pain. He flicked the switch on the steering column that controlled the radio, increasing the volume so that it blotted out the laughter and chatter from the back seat. Immediately Cissie-Rose gave him an approving smile, and wetted her already over-glossed lips with the tip of her tongue. When he failed to respond she leaned towards him, very deliberately placing one manicured hand high up on his thigh.

'I am so glad you did that,' she told him huskily. 'Tilly's voice is quite shrill, isn't it? I suppose it must be her English accent. It was beginning to make my head ache. How long have you known one another, did you say?'

'I didn't,' Silas answered her coolly.

'She's a very lucky young woman to have landed a man like you in her bed.'

'The luck's all mine,' Silas responded.

Cissie-Rose was coming on to him strongly, and he

recognised that if he encouraged her she might provide him with a shortcut to the information he needed. But his immediate rejection of the idea was so intense it was almost as if he was recoiling physically and emotionally from the thought of sharing the kind of intimacy he had begun with Tilly with anyone else. A physical and an *emotional* recoil? Just what exactly did that mean? If he carried on like this he would soon be telling himself he felt guilty about what he was doing, and he couldn't afford that kind of self-indulgent luxury.

Even when they had reached town and parked the car, Cissie-Rose was still trying to claim Silas's attention, leaving Tilly to help her two sons out of the car, checking that they were well wrapped up against the icy cold wind whipping down Segovia's narrow streets.

The ground underfoot was covered in snow and ice, and—predictably—Cissie-Rose clutched at Silas's arm. The two boys positioned themselves either side of Tilly, clinging to her so trustingly that she didn't have the heart to say anything.

Silas looked grimly at Tilly's bent head and wondered why she had this ability to make him feel emotions he didn't want to feel, and how she managed to activate a protective, almost possessive male instinct in him that no other woman had ever touched. It certainly wasn't what he wanted to feel. Yet, watching her now with the two boys, he was conscious of a sharp sense of irritation that they were there, fuelling his need to have her to himself.

'Tilly and I have rather a lot to do, so we might as well split up, Cissie-Rose, and let you and the boys get on with your shopping. How long do you think you'll need?' he asked, lifting his arm to check his watch so that Cissie-Rose was forced to remove her hand from it.

'Oh! I thought we could all shop together,' she protested. 'It would be so much more fun that way. Tilly and I could do some girly stuff, and you guys could go have a soda or something, and then we could all meet up for lunch.'

This was Cissie-Rose in smiling 'good mom' mode, Tilly recognised, as the boys looked uncertainly at their mother.

'You're okay with that, aren't you, you guys?' Cissie-Rose appealed to her sons. 'Or would you prefer to stay with Tilly.'

Witch! Tilly thought with uncharacteristic venom. Tails you win, heads I lose.

'We want to stay with Tilly,' the two boys chanted together.

Immediately Silas shook his head. 'Sorry, boys, but I'm afraid you can't.'

The vehemence in his voice made Tilly curl her toes in excited reaction to the intimacy his determination to have her to himself suggested. 'Tilly and I have some Christmas shopping to do. And she *is* my fiancé.' The look he was giving her made her face burn, and Cissie-Rose's expression changed to one of acid venom as she glared at Silas.

She would make a bad enemy, Tilly realised when she saw the look in her eyes.

Silas didn't seem too concerned, though. Ignoring Cissie-Rose's obvious hostility to his suggestion, he continued calmly. 'I don't want to linger in town, Cissie-Rose. The weather forecast they gave out on the way over didn't sound very good.'

'Oh. I see. Well, okay, then.'

It was obvious that Cissie-Rose did not think it was anything like okay at all, Tilly realised, feeling uncomfortable as she saw the furious look the other woman was giving her.

'Look, why don't we meet back here in, say, a couple of hours?' Silas suggested. 'Here's a spare key for the car in case you get back before us. That way you won't have to stand around waiting in the cold. And I'll give you my mobile number just in case you need it. Ready, Tee?'

Tilly disengaged herself from the boys and hurried towards him, hating herself for being so grateful both for the supporting arm he slid round her and the warmth of the smile he gave her.

'It's okay. You can let go of me,' she told him slightly breathlessly five minutes later. 'Cissie-Rose can't see us now.'

'You are my fiancé; we're passionately in love. We're hardly going to walk feet apart from one another, are we? And you never know—we could bump into Cissie-Rose anywhere. It is only a small town. Besides,' Silas told her softly, 'I don't want to let go of you.'

Was it necessary for him to go to these lengths? He had established himself now as Tilly's fiancé. And after last night… After last night, what? It was because of last night that he had been left with this ache that had somehow taken on a life force of its own. This ache that right now…

What was Silas thinking? Tilly wondered. What was

making him look so distant and yet at the same time, now that he had turned his head to look at her, so hungry for her?

When he reached for her Tilly didn't even try to resist. He turned her around to face him in the shelter of an overhanging building, where no one could see them, and then pressed her back against the wall, covering her body with the warmth of his own.

He whispered into the softness of her parting lips, 'I know there are any number of reasons why I shouldn't be doing this, but right now I don't want to know about them. Right now, right here, what I want, *all* I want, is you, Tilly.'

Why was he doing this when he didn't have to? Why ask himself questions that he couldn't answer? Silas answered himself as he gave in to the need that had been aching through him since last night and bent his head to kiss Tilly.

This wasn't a sensible thing for her to be doing, Tilly warned herself. But suddenly being sensible wasn't what she wanted. What she wanted was… What she wanted was Silas, she admitted. And she stopped thinking and worrying and judging, and simply gave herself over to feeling, as they clung together, kissing like two desire-drugged teenagers, oblivious to everything and everyone else.

What followed should have been an anticlimax. Instead it was the start of the most wonderful few hours Tilly had ever had.

The small town was picture-perfect, with its honey-coloured stone houses covered in pristine snow—which, thankfully, had been swept off the streets. Silas insisted on keeping her arm tucked through his. And when at one point he simply stopped walking and looked at her, she could feel her cheeks turning pink in response to the look in his eyes.

'Don't do that,' she protested.

'Don't do what?'

'Look at me like that.'

'You mean like I want to kiss you again?'

'This is crazy,' Tilly said, shaking her head.

'Isn't that what people are supposed to say when they start to fall in love?'

Silas could see the shock in her eyes. He could feel that same shock running through his own body. What the hell was he doing, dragging love into the situation? He felt as though he had suddenly become two people whose behaviour was totally alien to each other—one of whom was saying that he never played emotional games with women, that he despised men who did, so why the hell was he using a word like "love", while the other demanded to know who had said anything about playing games? It was as though he was at war with himself. He tried to shake off the feeling that they had somehow strayed into a maze and come up against a blank wall.

'There's a coffee shop over there. Shall we go in and have a drink?' Anything to try and get himself back to normal.

Tilly nodded her head in relief. Now that she was free of the spell the intimacy of Silas's sexuality seemed to cast over her, she was shakily aware of how vulnerable she was. Things were moving far too fast for her. She wasn't used to this kind of situation. And somehow she couldn't quite get her head round accepting that Silas could actually *mean* what he was saying. It was too much too soon. But she wanted him. She couldn't deny that.

She drank the coffee Silas ordered for them both, and tried to focus on the people hurrying up and down the street outside the window rather than on Silas, as she secretly wanted to do. In fact right now what she wanted more than anything else was just to be able to look at him, to absorb every tiny physical detail while she tried to come to terms with what was happening.

Silas watched her. He felt as though he could almost read her thoughts. She didn't know whether to believe he was being honest with her. He could sense it in every small action she made. She wanted him; he knew that. But he could see that she was dubious about accepting the immediacy of the situation.

They had both finished their coffee. Silas stood up. 'I'll be back in a minute,' he said, nodding his head in the direction of a pharmacy on the other side of the street.

Tilly didn't catch on immediately, but when she saw the green cross over the building her face burned, and she made an incoherent sound of assent, using Silas's absence to go to the ladies' room to comb her hair and replace the lipstick he had kissed off earlier. By the time she emerged, Silas had returned and was waiting for her.

'I think I'd better buy your mother a small Christmas

gift, but I'm going to need you to advise me,' he said, steering her in the direction of a small gift shop with a mouthwatering window display. To Tilly's relief he didn't say a word about his visit to the pharmacy.

The gift shop proved to be a treasure trove of the unusual and the enticing, and Tilly found presents for each of the children. It was only when the small ornamental jewellery box Silas had bought for her mother was being giftwrapped that Tilly looked at her watch and realised that it was almost two hours since they had left the car park.

'We ought to be heading back,' she warned Silas.

'Yes, I know. Not that I'm particularly looking forward to the return trip with Cissie-Rose. She can sit in the back this time—car sickness or not,' he told Tilly, before adding in a warmer tone, 'I thought you handled the boys very well, by the way. You obviously like children.'

'Yes. And it's just as well, really. My father remarried and has a second younger family, and all my mother's exes have children—most of whom also have children of their own now.'

'The ramifications of the modern extended family can be quite complicated,' Silas observed as he took the package from the shop assistant.

As they stepped out in the street, Tilly gave a small gasp of delight. 'It's snowing!' she exclaimed.

'Martin warned me that heavy snow had been forecast.'

This time it was Tilly who automatically slipped her arm through his as they headed for the car park.

A clock was just striking the hour when they reached it, making their way through the parked vehicles to where Silas had left the four-wheel drive.

But when they got to where it should have been there was only an empty space that the snow was just beginning to cover.

CHAPTER EIGHT

'SILAS, someone must have stolen the car,' Tilly exclaimed, shocked.

'I doubt that.' There was a grimness in his voice that made Tilly look uncertainly at him. His mobile had started to ring and he removed it from his pocket, flicking it on, while Tilly moved discreetly out of earshot so as not to seem as though she were listening in.

'That was Cissie-Rose,' Silas announced, coming over to her. 'Apparently she'd had enough of Segovia, and the boys were cold and tired, so she decided to take the car and drive back without us.'

Tilly's face revealed her shocked disbelief.

'You mean she's left us here with no way of getting back to the castle?'

'I mean exactly that,' Silas agreed curtly.

'But why on earth would she do that?'

Silas suspected that he knew the answer. Cissie-Rose had made it plain that she was offended because he hadn't responded to her sexual overtures on the drive to Segovia, and this, he suspected, was her way of paying him back for his refusal to play along. This development was a complication he hadn't allowed for, he admitted. From the point of view of achieving his purpose in coming to Spain, it made sense to cool things down with Tilly. He could continue to play the role of her fiancé while at the same time discreetly making use of Cissie-Rose's none-too-subtle hint that she was open to a flirtation with him, since Cissie-Rose would undoubtedly provide him with a more direct route to Art's confidences than Tilly. With his research at stake he wasn't in a position to allow himself the luxury of moral scruples. He had a duty to reveal the truth.

But no duty to live it?

If he had to choose between vindicating those who had worked to reveal the truth about Jay Byerly and sacrificing Tilly's good opinion of him, he had to choose the greater need. And what about Tilly herself. What about her need and her feelings?

Silas could feel anger with himself boiling up inside him. He was dragging issues into the equation that did not need to be there. He and Tilly were sexually attracted to one another. There was no logical or moral reason why, as two consenting adults, they shouldn't be free to explore that mutual sexual attraction, and no reason either why they should not enjoy a shared relationship. It didn't need to affect his original purpose in coming here.

And it could be over as quickly as it had started. Was that what he hoped for and wanted? Because he didn't want to have to see the look in Tilly's eyes if she discovered the truth?

There was no point in telling her. His original

decision had been made before he had met her, and had nothing whatsoever to do with her. Semantics, Silas warned himself. And they weren't enough to take away the acid sour taste of growing dislike of his dishonesty.

Tilly looked up at the sky, from which snow was falling increasingly heavily and fast. Icy prickles of anxiety skidded down her spine. She was pretty sure that Cissie-Rose had acted out of spite and selfishness, but she didn't want to run her down in front of Silas and end up sounding catty and judgemental. Besides, she had more important things to worry about than complaining about what Cissie-Rose had done. Like worrying about how on earth they were now going to get back to the castle.

'Perhaps we should ring the castle and ask if someone could come and collect us?' she suggested to Silas.

He shook his head. 'It will be much simpler if we try and organise a car from this end. I noticed a car-hire place earlier.'

Half an hour later, there was a grim look on Silas's face as he was told that the earliest anyone could provide them with a car would be the following day.

The snow was now falling thick and fast.

'There's nothing else for it, I'm afraid,' he told Tilly. 'We're going to have to spend the night here in town. I noticed a couple of hotels when we were walking round.'

What Silas said made good sense, but Tilly's heart had sunk further with every word. She too had noticed the hotels as they'd walked past them. Both of them had looked very exclusive, and would therefore be expensive. Knowing she was on a limited budget, she had deliberately left her credit card at the castle, in case she was tempted to use it, and all she had in her bag was a small amount of currency that would be nowhere near enough to pay for even one hotel room, never mind two and the cost of a hire car.

'It does make sense to stay here,' she agreed. 'But I'm afraid we're going to have to find somewhere inexpensive, Silas. You see, I didn't bring my credit card with me...'

Silas could see how uncomfortable and worried she was. 'It's my fault we've been stranded here,' he told her calmly. 'I suppose I should have guessed that Cissie-Rose might play this kind of trick on us. Don't worry about the cost of the hotel and the car hire. I'll pay for them.'

'You can't do that,' Tilly objected. 'Both those hotels looked dreadfully expensive. It wouldn't be fair. They could cost you more than I've paid the agency...'

'It's okay. Calm down. The agency always give us emergency cover money. I daresay they'll reclaim it from you once we get back home,' he fibbed, adding briskly, 'Look, we either book in somewhere or we hang around for hours in the hope that Martin can be called in from his half-day off to come and collect us.'

His reference to Martin being on his half-day off had the effect on Tilly's conscience he had known it would. Immediately she shook her head and protested, 'Oh, no, we can't do that. It wouldn't be fair.'

'And it won't be fair to us either, if we stand here and freeze to death—will it?' he said, taking hold of her arm and firmly turning her round in the direction of the town.

'It's going to look very odd if we book in without any luggage,' Tilly warned him.

'Not in these weather conditions. They're probably used to travellers getting stranded.'

Ten minutes later they were standing in the snow outside one of the hotels Tilly had noticed. It looked even more exclusive close up than she had thought when she'd seen it earlier.

'We can't book in here,' she protested to Silas.

'Of course we can,' he said, ignoring her inclination to hang back and nodding his head in acknowledgement of the uniformed doorman holding open the door for them.

Although he had a relatively well-paid job, Silas wasn't dependent on it financially. His maternal grandparents had been wealthy, and Silas, as their only grandchild, had inherited the bulk of it. Ordinarily he chose to live on what he earned, but he was perfectly comfortable in the kind of moneyed surroundings they were now entering—as Tilly noted when she stood back while he approached the reception desk.

Within five minutes he had returned to her side, explaining, 'They're pretty fully booked, because of the time of year, but they can give us a suite and they'll sort out a hire car for us for the morning.'

'A suite? But that will cost the earth!' Tilly protested.

'It's all they had left,' Silas told her grimly. 'We'd better go up and make sure it's okay. Then, since we won't be returning to the castle until tomorrow morning, I think that we might as well find somewhere to have a late lunch and explore the rest of the town.'

He didn't want to admit even in his most private thoughts how torn he was between the sheer urgency of his physical desire for Tilly and the cautionary voice inside him that was warning him that if he had any sense he would keep Tilly at arm's length, instead of increasing the intimacy between them—for her sake as well as his. *Her* sake? When exactly had he started to care about wanting to protect her?

Tilly nodded her head in approval of Silas's plan. The lift had arrived, and Silas stood back to allow her to precede him into it, his hand resting against her waist in the kind of discreet but very proprietorial gesture powerful men tended to use towards their partners. She could feel an almost sensual warmth spreading out from where he was touching her to envelop virtually the whole of her body. It made her want to move closer to him, so that she could absorb even more of it. In fact it made her want to do things she would normally have a run a mile rather than do…such as lifting her face for his kiss the second the lift doors closed.

How could it have happened that she had become so desperate for his touch that she felt like this? She had grown used to thinking of herself as the kind of woman who scorned such things as passionate embraces in lifts. But now she felt achingly disappointed because Silas was not making any move towards her at all.

Getting into the lift with Tilly instead of using the stairs had been a serious misjudgement, Silas admitted. The small enclosed space meant he was standing close enough to Tilly to be surrounded by the woman-scent of her skin and hair. They drew him to her with the irresistible pull nature had expressly designed them to have. Standing this close to her made him want to stand even closer still, and to do far more than just stand with her. He wanted to take her and lay her down beneath him, so that he could explore and savour every delicious inch of her, starting with the toes he had watched her curl up in sexual reaction to him, and moving all the way up to her mouth.

The lift jolted to a halt, its doors opening. Tilly stepped out into an elegant corridor and waited for Silas to join her.

'We're in here,' he told her, indicating a door to their right and going to open it.

Silas had said he'd booked them a suite, and she had assumed this meant they would have two bedrooms and their own bathroom, Tilly thought as she stood in the middle of the smart sitting room of the suite. She said uncertainly, 'There's only one bedroom.'

'I know, but, as I said, this suite was all they had left. And, after all, it isn't as though we aren't already sharing a bed.' Something about the words 'already sharing a bed' had an effect on her emotions Tilly wasn't sure she was ready for. They made them sound so intimate, so partnered—almost as though they were not just having a relationship but were already a couple.

'If you aren't happy with this we could always try the other hotel,' Silas offered.

Tilly shook her head. 'That would be silly. We might not get in.'

Ordinarily she would have been thrilled to be staying somewhere so upmarket and elegant. The building in which the hotel was housed was centuries old, but somehow the designers had managed to complement the age of the building by teaming it with the very best in modern design, rather than create a discordant mismatch.

Their suite comprised a sitting room, a bedroom, a state-of-the-art limestone bathroom, and a separate dressing room. While the bedroom overlooked the street, the sitting room overlooked a private courtyard garden to the rear of the hotel, which Tilly guessed would be used as an outdoor dining area in summer but which right now was covered in inches of snow.

'I just wish I had the clothes with me to do this place justice,' Tilly admitted ruefully.

At least she was wearing her good winter coat and her equally good leather boots. She'd become a fan of careful investment dressing with her first job in the City, even though her mother frequently complained that her choice of immaculately tailored suits was dull and unsexy. The black coat she was wearing today was cut simply, and her leather boots were neat-fitting and smart, just like the knee-length skirt she had on underneath the coat, and the plain cashmere sweater she was wearing with it. Thank heavens she had decided at the last minute this morning, after mentally reviewing the impression she had gained of the town the day before, not to wear jeans.

'I really ought to ring my mother and explain what's happened,' she told Silas.

'Why don't I ring Art instead?' he suggested.

Tilly looked at him. She had a good idea that he wanted to speak to Art and make his feelings about Cissie-Rose's behaviour very clear.

'There's no point in making a fuss about what's

happened. Cissie-Rose will have calmed down by the time she gets back to the castle, and I don't want Ma to get herself upset.'

'You mean you think we should let Cissie-Rose get away with it?' Silas shook his head. 'No. When we tolerate that kind of behaviour in others, we allow them to continue with it. She needs to know that what she did is not acceptable.'

'I know what you're saying, but it's obvious that Art adores his daughters.' And equally obvious—to her at least—that her mother was living in mortal fear that they might somehow persuade their father not to marry her. So, no matter how much she might agree with Silas, her concern for her mother made her want to protect her. 'I do agree in principle,' she acknowledged. 'But since we're all going to be spending the next week together at the castle, I think on this occasion it makes sense to turn the other cheek, so to speak.'

'Giving in to Cissie-Rose won't prevent her from trying to oust your mother from her father's life, you know.'

Tilly wasn't quite quick enough to conceal from him how much his awareness of her private thoughts had caught her off-guard.

'Did you really think I wouldn't guess why you wanted Cissie-Rose spared the repercussions of her nastiness? It wasn't hard to work out what you were thinking. After all, Cissie-Rose hasn't given you any valid reason to want to protect *her*.'

'I feel so sorry for her sons. She uses them like…'

'Bargaining counters?' Silas supplied astutely.

'Well, I wouldn't have put it as directly as that. I

meant more that she uses them to highlight and underline her own role as a good mother.'

'Oh, yes, she does that all right. But you can bet your City bonus that should the need arise she would have no compunction whatsoever about reminding Art where the future lies and who it lies with—and that won't be your mother.'

'You don't think that Art will marry Ma, do you?' Tilly said.

'He'd be doing her a favour if he didn't,' Silas responded harshly. 'I assumed at first that your mother was marrying him for the financial status and privileges marriage to him would give her, but it's obvious that she doesn't have the—'

'Careful,' Tilly warned him. 'Especially if you were thinking of using words such as *intelligence*, *nous* or *astuteness*.'

'You're right. It wouldn't be fair to use any of them in connection with your mother,' Silas responded, with such a straight face that it took Tilly several seconds to recognise that he was deliberately teasing her.

'Oh, you,' she protested, picking up one of the cushions from the sofa and throwing it at him.

He caught it easily, but when he threw it back down on the sofa he said menacingly, 'Right...' and began to walk purposefully towards her.

Tilly did what came naturally, and took to her heels.

Silas, as she had known he would, caught her in seconds and with ease, turning her round in his arms to face him as she laughed and pretended to protest.

This wasn't what he had allowed for at all, Silas acknowledged as he felt the heavy slam of his heart in his chest wall and the flood of awareness it brought with it. 'This is completely crazy—you know that, don't you?' he heard himself saying thickly.

'What's crazy?' Tilly asked.

'Us. What's happening between us. *This*,' Silas answered.

Tilly knew that he was going to kiss her, and she knew too how much she wanted him to. So much that she was already standing on tiptoe so that she could wrap her arms around his neck to speed up the process.

Beneath his mouth she gave a soft sound of pleasure when he slid his hands inside her coat and then pulled her top free of her skirt, so that he was touching her bare skin. His hands were warm, their strength somehow underlining her own female weakness. She wanted to give herself over completely to his touch and his hold, and to know that he would keep her safe within that hold for ever. His hands moved further up her back, slowly caressing her skin, his thumbs probing the line of her bra, making her shudder in recognition of just how much she wanted to feel his hands cupping her breasts, stimulating her already tightening nipples with the urgent tugging demand of his fingers. In fact her desire was so great she had to stop herself from reaching out and guiding his hand to her breast.

Silas, though, had no such inhibitions, and openly moved against her so that she could feel his arousal. He wanted her as much as she did him.

Or did he? Was he just pretending to want her because he thought it was what she wanted? Was the kindness and the intimacy he was showing her nothing more than a cynical act? He had accused her of hiring him for sex. She had vehemently denied it. But what if he hadn't believed her?

Frantically, Tilly started to push him away.

Silas's immediate and very male reaction was to keep her where she was. He was already strongly aroused, and his body and his experience were both telling him that she wanted him just as much as he did her. But he could also see the agitation and panic in her eyes, and he knew it was *that* he had to respond to, not his own desire. Unwillingly, he let her go.

It was her old fear of getting out of her emotional depth as much as the current situation that had led to her blind, panicky decision to put an end to the growing intimacy of Silas's caresses, Tilly admitted. She shivered slightly, already missing the physical warmth of Silas's body. The trouble was that she simply wasn't used to this kind of sexual intimacy and intensity. And it scared her. Or rather her increasing hunger for Silas scared her. She had fought so hard against the danger of falling in love and giving herself to someone, of allowing herself to be vulnerable to them emotionally. And yet now here she was, virtually ready to throw away all that effort, ready to ignore everything she had warned herself about, to break down all the protective barriers she had set in place to guard herself simply because of Silas. A man she had only known a matter of days. Known? She didn't know him, did she?

'Are you going to tell me what's wrong, or do I have to guess?'

The formidable determination in Silas's voice made her whirl round to look at him.

'There isn't anything—' she began.

But he cut ruthlessly through the platitudes she would have mouthed, shaking his head and stating curtly, 'Of course there's something. You're no Cissie-Rose, Tilly. You aren't the game-playing type. You want me.'

'Yes,' she agreed, as lightly as she could. 'But, since I'm already heavily in debt to you for the cost of this suite, I didn't think it was a good idea to put even more pressure on my bank account by letting you think— Silas!' she protested shakily.

He had crossed the distance separating them so quickly that she had barely seen him move, never mind had time to take evasive action. And now he was holding her arms in an almost painful grip, looking at her as though he wanted to physically shake her, and with such a blaze of passion in his eyes…

'If you are actually daring to suggest what I think you are…'

She had never seen such anger in a man's eyes— and yet oddly, instead of frightening her, it actually empowered her.

'You were the one who accused me of wanting to hire a man for sex,' she reminded him fiercely.

'You're making excuses,' Silas said dismissively. 'I consider myself to be a pretty good judge of character, and I've spent enough time with you now to know that my first assumption was incorrect. You didn't push me away because you thought I'd be demanding payment from you, Tilly. We both know that.' Abruptly his eyes narrowed, and he continued softly, 'Or was it perhaps that you were afraid that the payment I might demand would be something other than money?'

What was he doing? Silas asked himself. Why hadn't he let Tilly just walk away from him? Because he wanted her so badly that he couldn't? And what exactly did *that* mean?

First he had been forced to deal with questions that came perilously close to admitting to a feeling of guilt, and now this. This feeling that he wanted to protect both Tilly and their burgeoning relationship from being damaged by the truth about why he was here.

Silas was getting far too close to the truth. Tilly wriggled uncomfortably in his grip, torn between a longing to lay her vulnerabilities bare to him and tell him how she felt and her deeply rooted habit of protecting her feelings from others.

'The situation we're in is promoting intimacy between us faster than I'm used to, so I suppose that I *do* feel a bit wary about it—and about you,' Tilly told him, covering her real feelings with careful half-truths, and hoping that he'd challenge her again.

Why was he doing this? Silas asked himself irritably. His behaviour was totally unfamiliar and irrational. He had agreed to stand in for Joe simply because acting as Tilly's fictional fiancé would give him the chance to get closer to Art Johnson, but now he was behaving as though the person he was most interested in getting closer to was Tilly herself. This kind of behaviour just wasn't him.

It wasn't that he was against committed relationships. It was simply that he hadn't as yet come up with any logical reason why he should want to be involved in one. He had always known that if the time ever came when he really believed he loved a woman he would want their commitment to one another to be exclusive and lead to marriage, but he had also decided that he didn't really believe that kind of love existed. So far he had been perfectly happy to substitute good-quality sexual relationships for the muddled emotional mess-ups that others called 'love', and he had never had any reason to want to push those relationships onto his sexual partners. In fact if anything he had always held off a little, and allowed them to be the ones to invite him to pursue them.

So what the hell was happening to him now? Because Tilly most certainly was not inviting him to do any such thing, and yet all he could think about was not just getting her into his bed and keeping her there but... But what? Getting her into his *life* and keeping her there?

Silas reminded himself again that his first duty was to his writing. He was too intelligent not to recognise that his determination to reveal the hidden scandal of the environmental damage caused by Jay Byerly's oil company had its roots in his childhood, his desire to support the cause his mother had espoused and in supporting had lost her life.

Millions of children suffered far worse childhood traumas than his own. He had been wanted. He had been loved. By both his parents. Those parents had been committed to one another and to him. And his father had done everything he could to ensure that the tragedy of his mother's death strengthened his own commitment to Silas rather than weakened it. When his father had re-married, nearly ten years after his mother's death, his introduction to his stepmother had been handled wisely and compassionately. Silas admired and liked his step-mother, and he genuinely loved his half-brother. He had no reason to feel hard done by in life.

But the loss of his mother had hurt. So how must Tilly feel, watching her mother enter into one bad rela-tionship after another? Tilly! How had she crept into his chain of thought? What the hell was happening to him?

'There is only one reason I would ever take a woman to bed,' he told Tilly harshly, as he pushed aside his inner thoughts and feelings. 'And that is my desire for her and hers for me.'

If only she was the kind of woman who had the courage to go up to him now and suggest boldly and openly that taking her to bed was exactly what he should do—and sooner rather than later. But she wasn't. And she was afraid to trust the over-excited eager need inside her that was trying to push her out of her relationship comfort zone. She had got so used to protecting her emotions that her sense of self and self-judgement no longer seemed to be working properly.

But she couldn't just walk away from a situation she had helped to create and pretend it wasn't happening. That was rank dishonesty, and if there was one thing she prided herself on and looked for in others it was total and complete honesty.

She took a deep breath, and then said to Silas, 'I know I gave you the impression that…that sex between us was something that could be on the agenda if it was what we both wanted. But…'

'But?'

'What happened last night wasn't…isn't… I just don't *do* casual sex,' she told him truthfully. 'Last night I got a bit carried away by the heat of the moment, so to speak, but now that we've both had time to reflect…'

'You've changed your mind?' Silas finished for her.

'I haven't changed my mind about finding you sexually attractive,' Tilly felt obliged to admit. 'But I have changed my mind about how sensible it would be to go ahead.'

She wanted him so badly, and yet at the same time she was afraid of taking the step that would take her from her emotionally secure present into a future that couldn't be guaranteed. Perhaps it was old-fashioned, but for her giving her body couldn't happen without giving something of herself emotionally. Modern men didn't always want that. She certainly didn't want to burden Silas with something he didn't want, and she didn't want to burden herself with an emotional commitment to a man who couldn't return it. It might be illogical, but she felt that by holding back sexually she was protecting herself emotionally.

Tilly was handing him the perfect get-out from his own unwanted temptation, and he would be a fool not to take it. So why was Silas even thinking about hesitating? Guilt wasn't a condition he liked experiencing. Neither were the feelings gripping him right now. Silas told himself that it wasn't too late for him to draw back and tell himself that he didn't really feel what he was feeling.

'My thoughts exactly,' he told her tersely. 'After all, one should never mix business with pleasure.'

Tilly felt his words like a physical blow, but she told herself that it was a good, clean blow she herself had invited, and that what didn't kill a person made them stronger. And she wanted to be strong to fight the very dangerous and intoxicating mix of emotions and desires Silas aroused in her.

'I'll give Art a ring to explain what's happened, and then I suggest we go and eat and explore the rest of the town.'

Why was she looking at him like that? Making him want to go to her and hold her and tell her… Tell her what? That he had lied to her?

His guilt lay so heavily on his conscience that it felt like a physical weight.

Tilly nodded her head. She was willing to agree to anything that meant she would be safe from the intimacy of being alone with him and the effect both it and he had on her.

It was his frustration at not being able to get on with his research that was fuelling his mood now, Silas tried to tell himself. Not Tilly, or how he felt about her.

CHAPTER NINE

TILLY looked uncertainly at her reflection in the shop mirror. Not because she was in any doubt about the dress she was trying on—she had known the moment she had seen it in the window that it would be perfect for her, and it was. No, her doubts were coming from the guilty conscience that made her remember that even though her mother might have apologised to her over the phone for what Cissie-Rose had done, and urged her to treat herself to 'something pretty' for which she would pay, Tilly knew that on her return to London she would have to find the money to pay back their hotel bill.

And if that wasn't enough to put her off the admittedly very reasonable cost of the little black dress that was clinging so lovingly to her curves, then she only had to point out to herself that she did not live the kind of lifestyle that actually required the wearing of little black dresses. But perhaps if she had one, another inner voice persuaded, she might accept more invitations where she could wear it.

She had seen the dress in the window of a small shop close to the hotel when she and Silas had walked past it earlier, on their way to find somewhere to have a late lunch. Afterwards she had made an excuse to slip away from Silas to have a closer look at it, telling him that she needed to buy a few personal items because of their overnight stay.

'It is perfect on you,' the sales assistant told her with a small smile. 'It's a dress that requires a woman to have curves. Its designer is Spanish, and it is a new range we have only just started to carry.'

It was just as well the other woman's English was better than her own Spanish, Tilly acknowledged, as she smoothed the fine-knit black jersey over the curve of her hip. The dress might be fitted, but it was also elegant, without any hint of tartiness or flamboyance. It was, in fact, the kind of dress one might spend a lifetime looking for and not find.

'With the right jewellery or a scarf it could be so versatile. See…' the shop assistant coaxed, bringing a chunky-looking costume jewellery necklace of black beads, glass drops and cream pearls tied with black silk ribbon and slipping it around Tilly's neck to show her what she meant. Then, putting the necklace on one side, she tied a brightly coloured silk scarf around Tilly's waist in the same way Tilly had noticed the elegant assistants in Sloane Street's Hermès shop wearing their scarves.

She needed something to wear for dinner at the hotel tonight, Tilly told herself, weakening.

Silas, who had been standing on the other side of the road watching her, reached into his pocket for his wallet. He had spent enough time on shopping missions with both his stepmother and his lovers to be able to recognise when a woman and an outfit were made for one another. If Tilly didn't go ahead and buy herself that dress in which she looked so intoxicatingly desirable then he would buy it for her. Even if he had to do so surreptitiously. He was, after all, her fiancé.

But why did he want her to have it? Because of the look of dazed disbelief he could see so plainly in her reflection as she stared at herself in the mirror, or because of what he was doing? Angrily he pushed aside his inner questioning of his motives. He had no option other than to use Tilly as the key to the locked door of Art Johnson's confidence.

'I'll take it,' Tilly told the waiting shop assistant.

'And the shoes?' the girl asked with a smile, indicating the pretty black satin evening shoes she had persuaded Tilly to try on with the dress.

Tilly looked down and then nodded her head, trying to control the almost dizzying sense of euphoria that was speeding through her. She had never thought of herself as the kind of woman who got excited about buying new clothes—but then she had never thought of herself as the kind of woman who got excited about the thought of having sex with a man she barely knew either, before Silas had come into her life.

Silas! He would be wondering where on earth she was. They had agreed to meet back at the restaurant where they had had lunch, and she still had another purchase to make. She gestured towards the pretty underwear set on display—a matching bra and boy-cut shorts in soft black and pale baby pink.

'It's another new range,' the saleswoman told her approvingly. 'It's been one of our most popular sellers.'

* * *

'Got everything you wanted?' Silas asked calmly when she met him outside the restaurant, as if she hadn't been half an hour longer than she'd said she'd be.

Silas had obviously been shopping himself, she noted, because he was carrying a very masculine-looking carrier bag.

'I didn't think the *maître d'* would be too pleased with me if I turned up for dinner tonight in chinos and a polo shirt,' he informed Tilly easily.

'I thought the same thing. Not about you. I meant about me,' Tilly said hurriedly. 'Well, I mean, I thought I'd better buy myself something to wear for dinner.' She was gabbling like a person on speed. Why? Surely not because just for a second, when she had watched the sales assistant packing up the rather more sexily cut bra than she would normally have chosen to wear and its accompanying briefs, she had had a sudden mental image of Silas removing her new dress to reveal them? And that, of course, was *not* the reason she had changed her mind about buying a pair of tights and had opted for hold-ups instead, was it?

It had stopped snowing while she had been in the shop, but now it had started again, falling so quickly and so thickly that she knew Silas was right when he told her to hold on to him. She still refused. 'I'll be perfectly all right.' What she really meant was that she would rather risk losing her balance in the snow than lose her heart in the intimacy of being physically close to him.

'Okay. Are you ready to go back to the hotel?' he asked. 'Or…?'

'I think we'd better, otherwise we're going to end up looking like walking snowmen.' She gave a small shiver, and then gasped as a crowd of young people came hurrying round the corner. One of them accidentally bumped into her, and Silas reacted immediately, grabbing her with both hands to keep her upright while she regained her balance.

Each time she was close to him the feelings she remembered from the time before came back—and more strongly, so that now her heart was racing, thudding clumsily into her chest wall and then bouncing off it, as though his body was a magnet to which it was helplessly drawn.

She lifted her head to thank him, but her gaze got as far as his mouth and then refused to go any further. It also refused to allow any of her other senses to override it. She was, Tilly recognised distantly, totally unable to do anything other than focus helplessly on Silas's mouth and long for the feel of it possessing her own. She had made her decision back in the suite. Had she? Was she sure about that? Given a second chance, would she make the same decision? Wasn't she already regretting the opportunity she had let slip from her through a fear that no longer seemed important compared with her desire? How had it come to this? That she should be so bewitched by the shape and cut of a pair of male lips to the extent that she yearned with everything in herself to reach out and touch them with her fingertip, to trace the shape of them and store it inside her memory.

The way Tilly was looking at him was making Silas aware of himself as a man in ways and with nuances he hadn't known were possible, he acknowledged. If she reached out and touched his mouth now, as she looked as though she was about to do, he knew that the touch of her fingertips against his lips would end up with the intimate caress of his mouth against the lips of her sex, by way of a hundred different kisses and touches, until his tongue probed for the hard bead of her clitoris so that he could bring her to orgasm and watch her pleasure filling her. He also knew that he couldn't let that happen. Not now that he had begun to see her as the woman she really was. How had it come to this? How had *he* come to this? How had it happened that he wanted her so badly and so completely?

'If we stay here much longer we'll freeze.' The harsh rejection in Silas's voice as he released her and turned away hurt far more than the icy sting of the blizzard-like snowfall, Tilly admitted, as he waited for her.

This time when he took a firm hold of her arm she didn't protest, but she did make sure that she kept as much space between them as she could—unlike the young couple she could see up ahead, with the girl tucked intimately into the boy's side, her head resting against his shoulder. Something inside her turned over painfully when they stopped walking, oblivious to everyone else, and the girl lifted her face to the boy's. Tilly heard her laugh softly as he brushed the snow from her face, and then stop laughing when he bent his head to kiss her. There was no need to guess or to question their feelings; they were enclosed in their own personal halo of delirious happiness and love.

CHAPTER TEN

'SO WHAT you're saying is that your responsibility within the bank is to find ethical investment opportunities for your client base?'

They were in the elegant restaurant attached to the hotel, having dinner. Tilly had told herself she was glad when Silas had suggested that he get ready first and then go down to the bar and wait for her there, so that she would have the suite to herself to get changed in privacy. It made so much more sense for them to do that. That way there would be no awkwardness or embarrassment, and no risk of any unwanted intimacy. And no risk either of her making a fool of herself, as she had done earlier in the street. She couldn't really blame Silas for taking the steps he had. Not after the way she had stared at his mouth as though…as though… Hurriedly she tried to redirect her thoughts and answer Silas's question.

'Yes. My department is responsible for finding ethical and ecologically safe investments for those clients who specify them. We don't earn the huge bonuses other sections of the City do, but I enjoy what I do, and I enjoy teaching the young bankers in my charge to think of ways in which to link profit to things that may benefit others.'

'Somehow I don't think you'd get someone like Art interested in your kind of portfolio,' Silas said cynically.

The waiter was refilling her wine glass and Tilly thanked him. She had been shocked when she had seen the prices on the menu, but Silas had told her not to worry because he had secured a deal for their room which had included dinner.

So far their meal had been delicious. After a seafood starter she had been tempted by the lamb for which the area was famous, and she had not been disappointed. She was beginning to feel slightly light-headed, though. The wine—her second glass—was obviously stronger than she had realised. Or was it Silas who was having such a dramatic effect on her? It was far too dangerous to take that line of thought any further. It would be safer to focus instead on the conversation Silas had instigated, even if right now recklessly she would much rather have been… What? In bed, with Silas making love to her? She shuddered so intensely that she had to put down her glass of wine.

'Cold?' Silas asked, frowning.

Hot was more like the truth, Tilly thought giddily. Hot for him, for his touch, his kiss, his body…

'If Art ever asks for my financial advice or input I'll be delighted to help him,' she told Silas, as lightly as she could. The truth was she suspected that Art, to judge from the interaction between the members of his family, probably had the kind of business ethics she most deplored. But her mother loved him, or at least believed that she did, and for her mother's sake she knew she would keep her own private opinions as exactly that.

'But you don't think that he will?' Silas knew that he was probing and pushing too hard—so hard, in fact, that it was almost as though he wanted to provoke an argument with Tilly. To offset the effect of seeing her in that dress that somehow managed to be both prim and incredibly sexy at the same time. He tried to ease his lower body into a more comfortable position. The table might be doing a good job of hiding the unwanted erection that was aching through him, but that didn't make its presence any easier for him to endure.

'You seem an unlikely candidate for ethical conservation,' he told Tilly abruptly, deciding to stop pushing her for a response to his earlier question.

Was there something in the air that was causing Silas to behave towards her so antagonistically? Tilly wondered miserably. Or was this simply his way of warning her that he wanted her to keep her distance from him?

'If that's some kind of dig at my mother,' she said, giving up on her earlier attempts to pretend that she wasn't aware that he was trying to needle her, 'just because she's fallen in love with Art it doesn't mean that she agrees with his opinions. As a matter of fact, my mother met my father at a fundraising event for Save the Children.' She wasn't going to tell him that her mother had attended the event thinking it was a charity ball. 'My father is a very committed conservationist; he and my stepmother run a small organic farm in Dorset.'

He could see her against that kind of background, Silas recognised. Free-range hens, a quartet of unruly

children, and probably a couple of even more unruly
goats. What locked his heart muscle, though, was that
he could see those children with a mixture of their
shared colouring and features. Him? With four children?
He frowned at his wine glass. He was skating on very
thin ice now, and what lay beneath it was deep and dark
and had the potential to change his whole world. Was
that what he wanted? Because if it wasn't he needed to
banish those kind of thoughts right now, and put something in their place that would remind him of all the
reasons why he needed to keep Tilly out of his life. Like
how guilty he was going to feel when he saw the look
in her eyes if she learned the truth. He couldn't afford
that kind of emotional involvement with Tilly.

'Finished?'

Tilly nodded her head. She had been toying with the
last dregs of the coffee they had been served half an hour
ago for so long that she was not really surprised by
Silas's question. But she was unnerved by it. By it and
by him, she admitted as she got to her feet on legs that
suddenly seemed unfamiliar and shaky.

With every step she took out of the restaurant and
along the corridor to the lift, the shakiness and the
mixture of longing and apprehension that accompanied
it grew. In a few minutes she would be alone with Silas
in their suite. And then she would be alone with him in
its bed… And then…

Tilly had to have one of the smallest waists he had ever
seen, Silas decided as he tried to distract his thoughts
from what was really on his mind by mentally measur-

ing it with his hands. And then, far more erotically, mentally allowing those hands to slide slowly down to the curve of her hips and up over her back, so that he could tug down the zip of her dress and encourage the fullness of her breasts to spill into his hands.

She and Silas were inside the lift. Tilly could hardly breathe she felt so on edge.

'I have to say that I find it hard to understand how someone who purports to be so keen on environmental ethics doesn't feel more inclined to take issue with the mindset of a man like Art Johnson—especially when her mother is going to marry him. Or does the fact that he is a billionaire excuse him?'

The lift had stopped, and Silas was getting out. Tilly was in shock from the unexpectedness and savagery of his verbal attack on her. She could feel the hot burn of tears at the backs of her eyes.

'No, it doesn't,' she told him fiercely as he opened the suite door for her. Walking past him, she went over to the window, unable to trust herself to look at him in case he saw how much his words had hurt her. 'I may not agree with his business ethics, but I have to think of my mother.' She spoke with her back to Silas, biting hard on the inside of her bottom lip as she felt the betraying tears escape and fill her eyes.

It had been hard for her the previous evening, not to speak out against some of the things that Art and his family had said, but she had warned herself that arguing with them would not change the way they thought, and could potentially make things even more difficult for her mother. She could end up being hurt.

But now *she* was the one being hurt, and the shock of discovering just how easily and lethally Silas's critical comments could hurt her was making it very difficult for her to find her normal calm resistance to the negative opinions of others. The problem was that Silas wasn't 'others'. Somehow he had managed to stride over the subtle defences she'd thought she had so securely in place and put himself in a position where she was vulnerable to him. Far too vulnerable. As her reaction now was proving.

Silas could see Tilly's reflection in the window. The sight of the tears she was battling to suppress caused him a physical pain that felt like a giant fist hammering into his heart. His reaction to her tears rocked his belief system on its axis, throwing up a whole new and unfamiliar emotional landscape within himself. He inspected it cautiously, whilst his heart hammered against his ribs. He scarcely recognised himself in what he had become. And he certainly didn't recognise the intensity of the emotions battling it out inside him. His guilt, his pain for Tilly's own pain, were raw open wounds into which he had poured acid. How could he have changed so dramatically and swiftly? He felt as though something beyond his own control had blasted a pathway within him, along which were travelling emotions and truths that only days ago had been wholly alien to the way he felt and thought.

He strode over to where Tilly was standing, driven there by him. She was so engrossed in trying to control her unwanted emotions that she didn't even realise he was there until she felt Silas's hand on her arm.

She stiffened immediately, in proud rejection of what she felt must be his pitying contempt for her vulnerability, and tried to turn away from him. But it was too late. He was turning her towards him. She'd thought she had herself under control, but a single tear betrayed her, rolling down her set face. She heard the muffled explosive sound Silas made, but she was battling too desperately to control her emotions to interpret it.

When he reached out and touched her face with his fingertips, catching the tear, she flinched and started to push him away, telling him fiercely, 'Don't patronise me. Just leave me alone.'

'Patronise you?' Silas groaned.

'Don't pity me, then, or feel sorry for me.'

'If I feel sorry for you it's because I'm burdening you with the weight of my need for you, Tilly.'

Tilly could hear his voice thicken with a mixture of pain and angry self-contempt that was so raw it made her throat ache. She looked up at him and saw the tension in his face. She could feel it too in the pressure of his hands on her arms, drawing her towards him.

'I want you with a compulsion I don't understand. You make me feel emotions I don't recognise. Being with you feels like walking through a landscape that is so alien to me I have no way of negotiating it, no inbuilt compass—nothing other than the need itself. You've made me a stranger to myself, Tilly. You've found something within me I didn't know was there.'

'I haven't done anything—' Tilly started to protest, but Silas stopped her, stealing the denial from her lips, tasting the *oh, please, yes* concealed within the *no* along with the salt of her tears as he kissed her and went on kissing her, until she was clinging to him, tears spilling from her open eyes, leaving them clear for him to read the emotions that were filling them.

'You know what's happening to us, don't you?' Silas demanded against her mouth as he kissed away the final tear.

What? Tilly wanted to beg him, but she was afraid to ask the question in case it spoiled the magic that had transported her to this new world, and broke the spell that was binding them together. So instead she whispered passionately to him. 'Show me! Don't tell me about it, Silas. Show it to me.'

CHAPTER ELEVEN

A HEARTBEAT later—or was it a lifetime?—Silas was undressing her in between fiercely possessive and demanding kisses, and she was undressing him. The room was full of the sound of rustling clothes, soft sighs and hungry kisses, as fabric slithered and slipped to the floor, and eager hands moved over even more eager flesh.

Somehow Silas had managed to remove all of his own clothes, as well as most of hers. Now, as he held her against him and slid his hands from her waist down over her hips, past her bottom and then up again under the fluted legs of her pretty new briefs, to cup her warm flesh and press her into his body, her own hand was free to give in to the unfamiliarly wanton demands of her emotions and explore the shape and texture of his rigid erection.

'Don't—' Tilly heard him protest thickly. But it was too late for him to deny the effect her touch was having on him. She had felt it in the savagely intense shudder of pleasure that had gripped and convulsed him.

His reaction gave her the courage to explore more intimately and to give way to the erotic urgings of her own senses. It both excited and aroused her to see and feel him responding so helplessly to her, so possessed by desire and need that he couldn't control the visibly physical pleasure she was giving him.

She could feel the heavy slam of his heart against her own body, its arousal mirrored by the uneven sound of his breathing in her ear as he held her and caressed her with growing passion. But when he stroked a shockingly erotic caressing fingertip down her back, beyond the base of her spine, it was her turn to moan in fevered arousal and melt into him.

Immediately she curled her hand around him, wanting to reciprocate the pleasure he was giving her, but Silas stopped her, telling her hotly, 'I can't let you do that. If I do…' She felt him shudder, and then shuddered herself when he told her, 'I want you so damn much that I can't trust myself not to come too soon if you touch me.'

'That works both ways,' Tilly protested breathlessly, squirming with heated pleasure under his exploratory touch, shocked by her own verbal boldness and yet at the same time acknowledging how much it meant to her to be able to be so open and natural with him about her sexual responsiveness.

How tame her imaginings in the shop as she had bought the new underwear seemed now, compared to the reality of what Silas's touch was actually doing to her. And as for her not touching him. How could she not when her need to do so was growing by the heartbeat? When she ached so badly to stroke her fingertips along the full length of his erection? She wanted to know every single nuance of the texture of its flesh. She wanted to explore the inviting slick suppleness of its pulse-racing male rhythm beneath her caress. She wanted…

She shuddered wildly under the erotic influence of her own thoughts, and then more wildly still when Silas stroked slowly all the way up her spine. His tongue-tip prised her lips apart and she admitted it eagerly, giving herself over completely to the thrusting passion of his kiss. His hand cupped her breast, and the heat inside her exploded in a firework display of shimmering pleasure. She caught his hand and pressed it fiercely against her breast as she moved rhythmically against him, every single part of her gripped by and focused on her longing for him.

Somehow, at some deep level, he had known it would be like this between them, Silas admitted as he lost the battle to control his response to Tilly's arousal. What she was doing to him was causing what felt like a huge unstoppable wave of aching intensity and need to power through him. He knew that he was helplessly unable to stop himself from succumbing to it and to her. He knew that he didn't even want to stop himself. And he knew that both of them were going to be overwhelmed by it, swept along together with only each other to cling to as the full power of what was happening to them possessed them. It was too late to stop it now, even if he wanted to. The openly urgent rhythmic movement of Tilly's body against his own was driving him over the edge of his self control.

'I want you,' he cried out in a raw voice. 'I want you more than I have ever wanted any other woman or will ever want any other woman ever again.' He heard the words, thick and half-crazed with emotion, being dragged from his throat, and he knew that they were true. He could see shock, delight and yearning in Tilly's eyes. He took her mouth in a kiss of fierce, consuming possession, picking her up and carrying her over to the bed.

Tilly moaned when Silas put her down, unable to bear even for a handful of seconds not to have him touching her or to be touching him.

She could see him kneeling over her, and she watched as he bent his head and traced a line of kisses down her body. His hands cupped and held her hips, and she shuddered when he anointed her hipbones in turn with slow, tender kisses and then moved lower. She could feel his fingers sliding through her ready wetness as he deliberately parted the outer lips of her sex. She could see him looking at her as he touched her.

Her flesh was flushed and swollen with arousal, making Silas ache to taste her, to feel the sharp shudders of her orgasm against his mouth. He wanted to slide his fingers through the wetness of her sex, between the fullness of the labia, and then part them so that he could stroke his tongue along the path made by his fingertip. He wanted to take the small responsive bead of her clitoris and caress it until he had brought her to the edge he had already reached, and then he wanted to slide slowly and deeply the full length of her, so that he was filling her, and she was holding him, and her flesh was taking him and using him for its pleasure, making that pleasure his own.

What he wanted, he recognised, was a degree of intimacy with her, a connection with her, a *completeness* with her that was outside any sexual experience he had ever had previously, or imagined he could want. Because what was happening for him wasn't something he only wanted to experience on a sexual level. What he wanted from her went way beyond that into a realm he had always thought more akin to make-believe and fiction than reality.

Tilly gave a small aching moan. Silas bent his head and parted her labia, stroking his tongue-tip the full length of her sex.

It was more than Tilly could stand. She cried out and dug her nails into his shoulders, clinging desperately to the edge of her own self-control.

'No,' she told him fiercely. 'Not yet. Not until you're inside me. That's how I want it to be, Silas.' Determined tears sprang into her eyes as she looked at him. 'It has to be both of us. I want *you*, Silas,' she insisted. 'I want you *inside* me. I want that so much.'

She felt him move, heard the brief rustle of a wrapper being opened and then discarded, and then blissfully he was holding her, kissing her, sliding his hands down to her hips and lifting her. Hungrily Tilly wrapped her legs around him, arching up eagerly to meet his first slow, sweet thrust into her.

Silas shuddered as he felt her muscles grip and hold him. Even this was a new kind of pleasure. Where he had previously known experience, with Tilly there was freshness, an untutored naturalness that was so much more erotic. Her body welcomed him joyfully and eagerly, offering all its pleasures to him, wanting him to take them, wanting him to thrust deeper and harder until he fitted her so well that they might almost have been one flesh.

Was *this* what love was? Silas wondered. Was *this* why he had always refused to believe in it before? Because he had been waiting for Tilly?

She cried out his name, her flesh gripping him, pulsing fiercely.

Through the fierce contractions of her orgasm Tilly felt Silas's final deep thrust as he joined her in the soaring ecstasy that was binding them both together and taking them to infinity.

Silas moved away from the window and looked towards the bed. It was nearly two o'clock in the morning, but he hadn't been able to sleep. He hadn't been able to do anything since they had made love except go over and over inside his head the now familiar journey that had led from his first meeting with Tilly to this. He felt as though his whole life had suddenly veered off course and gone out of his control. How was it possible for him to have changed so much so quickly? How was it possible for him to feel so differently?

He made his way back to the bed. Not being within touching distance of Tilly made him feel as though a part of him was missing, that he was somehow incomplete.

As he slid back the duvet he realised that she was awake.

'You know what's going on, don't you?'

'I think so, and it isn't something I wanted to happen,' Tilly answered, trying to make her voice sound light and careless but hearing it crack as easily as he'd cracked apart the protective casing she had put around her heart.

'Falling in love wasn't exactly on my agenda either,' Silas told her dryly.

'Perhaps if we try really hard we can stop it.'

There was enough light from the moon for her to see the cynically amused look Silas was giving her. 'Like we've already tried once tonight, you mean?' he derided, causing Tilly to give a small shiver.

'Silas, I don't want to love you. I don't want to love anyone. Loving someone means being hurt when they stop loving you.'

'I won't stop loving you, Tilly. I couldn't.' It was, Silas recognised, the truth.

'This is crazy,' Tilly whispered, but she knew that her protests meant nothing and that her own emotions were overwhelming her.

'Love is crazy. It's well known that it's a form of madness.'

'Maybe it's just the sex?' she suggested. 'I mean…'

Silas shook his head.

'No, it isn't just the sex,' he assured her. 'You can trust me on that.'

'There can't be love without trust. And honesty,' Tilly whispered solemnly.

This was all so new to her, and so very precious and vulnerable. Acknowledging her feelings felt like holding a new baby. Her heart did a slow high-dive. A baby. Silas's baby.

Trust and honesty. Silas reached for Tilly. He was going to have to tell her the truth about himself, and his reason for taking Joe's place.

But not tonight. Not now, when all he wanted to do

was hold her and kiss her and feel the responsive silky heat of her body, taking him and holding him, while he showed her his love.

Tilly glanced anxiously at Silas. He had hardly spoken to her as he drove them back to the castle, and whatever he was thinking his thoughts didn't look as though they were happy ones.

'Second thoughts?' she asked him lightly.

'About the wisdom of returning to the castle? Yes. About us? No,' Silas answered her truthfully. 'What about you?'

'I rather think I've made it obvious how I feel.' They had made love again before breakfast, and now her body ached heavily and pleasurably with an unfamiliar, satisfied lassitude. She touched the comfortable weight of the ring on her left hand and then coloured self-consciously when she saw the gleam in Silas's eyes.

'I wish we could go back to London and get to know one another properly, instead of having to go back to the castle,' Tilly admitted. 'And I can't help worrying about my mother. It's obvious that Art's family doesn't want him to marry her.'

'My guess is that if they don't manage to break them up before they marry, they'll make her life hell afterwards. To be honest, I'm surprised she can't see that for herself.'

'Ma only sees what she wants to see,' Tilly told him. 'She can be very naive like that. I just don't want her to be hurt. When her last marriage broke up she was desperately unhappy. It was the first time she hadn't been the one to end things. If Art decides not to go ahead with the wedding, I don't know what it will do to her. Ma's one of those women who doesn't feel she's a viable human being unless she's got a man in her life.' Tilly smiled ruefully. 'That's probably more than you want to know. I'm sorry. But this is the first time I've felt close enough to someone to be able to be talk honestly about how I feel without thinking I'm being disloyal.'

'What about your father?'

'Oh, I love Dad, of course. But he disapproves of Ma, and they don't see eye to eye. I'd feel I was letting her down if I told him how much I worry about her, and why. They were so unsuited—but that's the trouble about falling in love, isn't it? You don't always know until it's too late that you aren't compatible. And sometimes even when you are it isn't enough.'

'Sometimes a couple meet and are fortunate enough to recognise that what they share goes far beyond mere compatibility,' Silas told her. 'Like soul mates.'

Tilly felt a fine thrill of the most intense emotion she had ever experienced run through her as he turned to look at her.

It moved her beyond words that Silas should say such a thing to her, almost as though he already knew how vitally important it was to her that the love growing between them should be perfect in every way.

And yet the closer they got to the castle the more she sensed that Silas seemed to be distancing himself from her, retreating to a place where he didn't want her to follow him. His answers to her efforts to make conversation became terse and unencouraging, giving her the message that he preferred the privacy of his own silence to any attempt to create a more intimate mood between them.

She told herself that she was being over-sensitive, and that what to her felt like a distancing tactic was probably nothing more than a desire to concentrate on his driving.

The closer they got to the castle the more Silas recognised the dual agenda he would now be operating under. From the outset he had been totally clear to himself about his purpose in stepping into Joe's shoes. He had told himself that deceiving a young woman he didn't know, while regrettable, would be justified by the exposure that would be the end result of his research. But he hadn't anticipated then that the impossible would happen and he would fall in love with Tilly.

Now that he had, his deceit had taken on a much more personal turn. He was now in effect lying by default to the woman he loved. He was lying to her about his real identity, the real nature of his work, the fact that he was using her as a cover to screen his own agenda.

For each and every one of those lies he had an explanation he believed she would understand and accept— after all, he had not set out with the deliberate intention of deceiving *her*. But the highly emotionally charged atmosphere of the castle, where they would be surrounded by Art and his family, was not, in Silas's opinion, the best place for him to admit totally what he had done, or his reasons—even though normally his first priority would have been to tell her the truth. For that he felt he— they—needed real privacy, and the security of being able to discuss the issue without any onlookers.

Knowing Tilly as he believed he did know her now, he couldn't ignore the instinct that told him that if his suspicions about Art's involvement in Jay Byerly's underhand dealings were confirmed, Tilly would at the very least want to warn her mother about the true nature of the man she was planning to marry. And if she did that, Silas thought it entirely likely that Annabelle would go straight to Art and beg him to deny the accusations being levelled against him.

Silas knew the last thing his publishers would want was to be threatened with a lawsuit by some expensive lawyer before his book was even written. And he certainly had no intention of putting himself in a position where the truths he had already worked so long to make public were silenced before they had been heard.

Tilly would, of course, be hurt, and no doubt angry when he told her the truth on their return to London, but he felt sure that once he had explained the reasons he had not been able to confide in her she would understand and forgive him. But while logically it made sense not to say anything to Tilly yet, loving her as he did meant that he wanted to share his every thought and feeling with her. It was for her own sake that he could not do it, he reminded himself. She was already doing enough worrying about her mother, a woman who in Silas's opinion ought to recognise how truly fortunate she was to have such a wonderful daughter.

Something was on Silas's mind, Tilly decided. In another few minutes they would be reaching the castle and the opportunity to ask him would be gone. She took a deep breath and said quietly, 'You look rather preoccupied. Is something wrong?'

Her awareness of his concern caused Silas to turn his head and look at her, and to go on looking at her. 'Yes,' he told her truthfully, adding, not quite so truthfully, 'The closer we get to the castle the more I wish I could snatch you up and take you somewhere we could really be on our own. There's so much I want to learn about you, Tilly. So much I want to know about you and so much I want you to know about me. And, selfishly, I want you all to myself so that we can do that. I've never thought of myself as a possessive man, but now I'm beginning to realise how little I really know myself—because where you are concerned I feel very unwilling to share you with anyone else.'

'Don't say any more,' Tilly begged. 'Otherwise I'll be pleading with you to turn around and drive back to the hotel.'

'The first thing I intend to do when we reach the castle is take you upstairs to our room and make love to you,' Silas told her thickly.

'I rather think that we'll be called upon to explain ourselves to Cissie-Rose first, and apologise for putting her to the trouble of having to drive back alone,' Tilly warned him wryly. 'She won't be happy to see us together, Silas.' That was the closest Tilly felt she wanted to go in telling Silas that she was aware that Cissie-Rose's interest in him was sexual and predatory.

'We don't owe her any explanations. She chose to leave in a strop and abandon us because I'd shown her that I wasn't interested in what she was offering.'

Tilly heard the hardness in his voice and winced a little.

Silas saw her small movement and shook his head. 'Don't waste your sympathy on her, Tilly. She doesn't deserve it.'

'I can't blame her for wanting you when I want you so much myself,' Tilly told him honestly.

Silas drove in to the courtyard, turning to look at her as he stopped the four-wheel drive to say softly, 'Promise me something, Tilly?'

Something? Her heart was so filled with love and happiness she wanted to promise him *everything*. 'What?' she asked instead.

'Promise me that you'll always be as honest and open with me as you are now. I love it when you tell me that you want me. And, just as soon as we get the chance, I intend to show you just how much.'

'Yes, poor Tilly needs to go and lie down. She started with a headache on the way back—didn't you, darling?'

Tilly shot Silas a reproving look, but he was too busy convincing her mother that she wasn't going to be well enough to emerge from their bedroom for at least a couple of hours.

'Well, I'm sure that Art and the boys won't mind keeping you company in the bar, Silas,' Annabelle told him, before turning to Tilly to say reproachfully, 'I wanted to show you my dress and the sketches Lucy has done for the flowers. Perhaps if you just took a couple of aspirin you wouldn't need to lie down…?'

Tilly wavered. She was so used to answering her mother's needs when she was with her, and Annabelle was looking at her like a disappointed child deprived of a special treat, making her feel wretchedly guilty. But Silas had reached for her hand and was very discreetly, but very sensually, caressing the pulse-point on the inside of her wrist. Her desire for him was turning her bones and her conscience to jelly.

She looked at her mother and lifted her free hand to her forehead. 'Silas is right, Ma.' she told her. 'I really do need to lie down.'

Five minutes later, when Silas locked the door to their room and leaned on it for good measure, taking her in his arms and drawing her very deliberately into the cradle of his hips so that she could feel his arousal, Tilly shook her head at him.

'I don't believe I've just done that. I've never lied to my mother before…'

'When there's a conflict of interests I'm delighted that you opted to choose me,' Silas teased her.

Tilly didn't respond to his smile as readily as he had expected. 'Loving someone shouldn't mean abandoning your own moral code. Telling my mother I had a headache when I haven't…'

'What would you have preferred to do? Tell her that we wanted to make love?'

Tilly exhaled in defeat. 'No,' she admitted. 'But it still doesn't make me feel good.'

'Maybe this will, though.'

Silas was teasing her with small, unsatisfying kisses that made her reach up for him and pull his head down to hers…

* * *

'You remember that TV show *Dallas*? Well, I'm telling you that was nothing compared with the reality of how the oil business was in my father's time. I started working in the family business straight out of school. My father said that was the best way to learn.' Art reached for his drink and emptied his glass, demanding, 'Come on Dwight, I thought you were playing bartender. Set them up again, will you?'

It was almost dinnertime, and to judge from his slurred voice and red face Silas suspected that Art had been drinking for the best part of the afternoon. He had greeted them affably enough when they had finally come downstairs dressed for dinner, and had then begun reminiscing about the early days of his family's oil business. Silas, sensing that this might be the breakthrough he needed, had encouraged him to keep talking by asking him judicially timed questions. He suspected from the bored expressions on the faces of Art's sons-in-law that they had heard all Art's stories before.

'I imagine you must have known all the big players in the old oil world?' Silas suggested casually.

'Sure did,' Art agreed boastfully. 'I knew 'em all.'

'Even Jay Byerly?'

'Yep. He was some guy, was Jay. He had a handle on just about everything that was goin' on.'

'I know that the shareholders voted him off the board of his own company in the end, but no one ever said why.' While they had been talking Silas had filled up Art's glass, making sure that he didn't fill up his own.

'For goodness' sake, no one wants to hear all those

old stories all over again. Poor Annabelle will be so
bored she'll change her mind about wanting to marry
you if you don't change the subject,' Cissie-Rose exclaimed with acid sweetness, sweeping into the room in
a dress that was more suitable for a full-scale diplomatic
reception rather than what was supposed to be a quiet
family dinner. 'You really mustn't encourage him,
Silas,' she added, giving Silas and Tilly the kind of
posed and patently artificial smile that showed off her
excellent teeth and the cold enmity in her eyes. 'Are you
really sure you're over your headache, Tilly?' she asked.
'Only, if you don't mind my saying so, you really don't
look well. There's nothing like a headache for making
a person look run-down.'

'Annabelle, why don't you girls go and talk wedding
talk in one of the other rooms?' Art suggested.

Tilly suspected that he had been enjoying basking in
the attention of Silas's good-mannered social questions,
and that he wasn't very pleased about Cissie-Rose's interruption. Although he wasn't exactly slurring his
words, he had had what to Tilly seemed to be rather a
lot to drink. Her doubts about the wisdom of her mother
marrying him were growing by the hour.

'Silas is just being polite, Dad. Why on earth should
he be interested in what happened over thirty years ago?
Unless, of course, someone's thinking of making a film
of Jay's life and you're hoping to be invited to try for
the lead part, Silas.'

Cissie-Rose's claws were definitely unsheathed now,
Tilly recognised. The other woman's cattiness made her
want to place herself physically in front of Silas to

protect him. Although the thought of Silas needing anyone defending him, least of all her, made her smile to herself.

'Ignore her, Silas,' Art instructed, giving his daughter a baleful look. 'You're right. There was a scandal Jay was involved in that threatened to blow him and the business sky-high. Luckily a few of the big old boys called in some of their debts and managed to get it all quietened down. Jay had been buying up oil leases and then—'

'Daddy, I don't think you should say any more,' Cissie-Rose interrupted her father sharply. 'It's all in the past now, anyway. Annabelle, I have to say that those sketches you were showing me for the flowers are just so pretty.'

It wasn't worth pushing Art any further, Silas decided. There would still be plenty of opportunity for him to pick up their conversation between now and the wedding on New Year's Eve. All he had to do was to make sure he mixed Art a jugful of extra-strong whiskey sour.

CHAPTER TWELVE

'CHRISTMAS EVE and I've already had the best present I could ever have,' Tilly told Silas emotionally.

They were in their bedroom getting ready for dinner, having spent the afternoon outside in the snowy garden playing with the children. Or rather Tilly had played with them while Silas had watched.

'It's kind of you to be so patient with Art, Silas. His face positively lights up when you walk in and let him tell his stories. He must be exaggerating some of them, though.' Tilly gave a small shiver. 'It seems wrong that men like Art should have had that kind of power and abused it the way they did.'

'Things are different now,' Silas agreed. 'But as for Art exaggerating what happened in the past...' He paused, all too aware of what he knew that Tilly did not. 'If anything,' he told her heavily, 'I suspect that Art is using rather a lot of whitewash to conceal some of what went on. Of course most of those who perpetrated the worst of the crimes are no longer around, but that doesn't mean the world doesn't need to know about them.'

'I'm so lucky to have met you,' Tilly said spontaneously. As he looked at her Silas felt his heart turn over inside his chest slowly and achingly as his love for her overwhelmed him. He reached for her hand, entwining his fingers with hers. He still found it hard at times to come to terms with the speed with which his life had changed so dramatically. And all because of one person.

'You're a saint for putting up with everything the way you have.'

'A saint! That's the last thing I am. In fact…' He had to tell her the truth, Silas decided, even though he knew that in doing so he would be subjecting her to divided loyalties. He was finding the deceit that he knew lay between them increasingly burdensome, plus he wanted to share his work with her now that he recognised that she was the most vital and important part of his life. Not involving her in what he was thinking and planning somehow felt like being deprived of the ability to work the way he wanted to do. He wanted her input and her support. He wanted her to know, to understand, and to accept what he was doing and why. He wanted, Silas recognised, to lay not just his heart but his very soul at her feet, so that she could know his every strength and vulnerability.

'Tilly, there's something—' he began, and then had to stop when there was a brief knock on their bedroom door and they both heard Tilly's mother calling out anxiously.

'Are you ready yet?'

'Almost,' Tilly answered, giving Silas a rueful look as she slipped from his arms and went reluctantly to open the door.

'Oh, you must hurry, then—because Cissie-Rose has

just rung through to our room to say she wants us all downstairs now, because she's got something important to say. Do you think she could possibly be expecting another baby, Tilly? Wouldn't that be lovely? Oh, you both look fine. Come on, we may as well go down together. Art's already down…'

'You said we'd have the buffet at seven,' Tilly reminded her. 'It's not even six yet.' She had been looking forward to having some private time with Silas before they had to join the others, but it was obvious that her mother wasn't going to leave without them.

He would tell Tilly later, when they came back up to their room, Silas promised himself. Preferably in bed, when he was holding her in his arms.

The familiar ache of his body for hers began to speed through him.

As they descended the stairs Tilly could hear the sound of familiar Christmas carols filling the hallway.

'I remembered to bring a CD of carols with me,' Annabelle told Tilly proudly. 'You used to love them so much when you were a little girl.'

The children were all in one of the smaller salons, watching television and trying to guess what Santa would be bringing them.

'There you are, Silas.' Art's voice boomed out. 'You're already a couple of drinks down on us.'

Tilly shook her head when Dwight offered to make her a drink, knowing from previous experience how strong it would be.

'So what's this news Cissie-Rose has for us, Dwight?' Annabelle asked excitedly. 'And where is she?'

'She's upstairs, taking a call.'

'If I know Cissie she's probably checking up on Hal to make sure he's got the wording of our pre-nup right,' Art joked.

Tilly looked anxiously at her mother, worrying about how she might be taking this less than romantic comment from her husband-to-be.

'Sorry to have to keep you all waiting, but I just wanted to make sure I had all my facts right before I came down.' Cissie-Rose paused dramatically in the doorway, and then slowly made her way over to Tilly. 'That's a mighty pretty engagement ring you're wearing, Tilly. Pity that neither it nor your engagement is real, though. In fact there isn't much that *is* real about you—is there, Silas? You see, Silas here isn't Tilly's fiancé at all. Are you, Silas?'

White-faced, Tilly reached for Silas's hand and drew on the warm comfort of its reassuring grip. This was awful—dreadful. And she could hardly bear to look at her mother. There was no doubt in Tilly's mind that this was Cissie-Rose's revenge on them for Silas's rejection. But Tilly still had no idea how on earth she had found out about them.

'Tilly thinks that Silas is an out-of-work actor she hired to come here and pretend to be her fiancé, so that we'd think she was a clean-living girl who was about to get married. Poor Tilly,' Cissie mocked, giving her a malicious smile. 'I really do feel sorry for you. Look at you, clinging on to him. How sweet. But I'm afraid there's worse to come. Isn't there, *Silas*? You see, Silas has been deceiving us all about the true purpose of his being here.'

'You don't understand,' Tilly protested fiercely. 'Yes, I admit that I originally hired Silas as an escort to accompany me here. But since we've been here…' She turned to Silas and gave him an anxious, pleading look that twisted his heart with pain.

'Since you've been here *what*?' Cissie-Rose taunted her triumphantly. 'He's taken you to bed and told you he wants you? Poor Tilly. I'm afraid it is *you* who don't understand. Because if that is the case then he's been lying to you as well as to us, and he's made a complete fool of you. There's only one thing he wants—only one reason he's come here—and it's got nothing to do with wanting you, has it, Silas? Or should I call you James? You see, everyone, this is *James* Silas Connaught.'

Tilly, who was battling to take in what Cissie-Rose was saying, saw the swift look of recognition Art and Dwight were exchanging, and something as cold as death started to creep through her veins like poison.

'Yes,' Cissie-Rose confirmed. 'The journalist who has been trying to get an interview with Dad for the best part of a year. That's right, isn't it, Silas? He must have thought it was his lucky day when you gave him the opportunity to use you, Tilly. *Of course* he took you to bed. He's known for being a journalist who always gets his story—aren't you, Silas?'

'No, that's not true. It can't be! There's been some mistake,' Tilly protested, white-faced. 'Please tell me this isn't true,' Tilly begged, turning to face Silas.

'Yes, there has been a *very* big mistake.' Cissie-Rose laughed unkindly. 'And you're the one who's made it, Tilly. Of course I saw right through you in a minute,

Silas,' she said. 'Which is why I've had Dad's lawyers doing some digging on you.'

'Silas?' Tilly begged. Why wasn't he denying what Cissie-Rose had said?

'Tilly, I can explain everything,' Silas told her fiercely.

Tilly stared at him. Where was the denial she had expected to hear? She couldn't bear to see what she was seeing in Silas's eyes. She wanted to run and hide herself away from the pain of it. She could feel herself starting to tremble violently inside. Nausea gripped her stomach, and a pain like none she had ever previously known tore at her.

'How could you? *How could you?*' She was still holding onto Silas's hand, but now she released it, not caring what anyone else might think as she ran towards the door and headed for the stairs.

She had to escape from their mockery and contempt. She had to escape from her own pain and humiliation. But most of all she had to escape from Silas. She wanted to lock herself away somewhere private and dark while she tried to come to terms with what she had just learned. She would have defended Silas against all accusations Cissie-Rose had made against him, just as she would have given him her trust and her belief unquestioningly if he had denied what Cissie-Rose had said. But instead he had shown her with his plea, and more tellingly with the look in his eyes, that everything Cissie-Rose had accused him of was true.

She could hardly think or reason logically for the pain that was swamping her. What a fool she had been— to believe his lies about falling in love with her. And no wonder he had been so keen to talk with Art. A mirth-less smile twisted her mouth. How ironic it was that she had been stupid enough, dense enough, besotted enough to praise him for his kindness. The pain tightened its grip, raking her emotions raw.

Silas caught up with her outside their bedroom door, refusing to let go of her when she tried to drag her wrist free of his imprisoning grip, bundling her inside the room and closing the door, enclosing them in what was for Tilly its tainted and treacherous intimacy.

'Let go of me,' she demanded.

'Not yet. Not until you've listened to me. I know you're upset, and I understand how you must feel—'

'How dare you say that to me? You know nothing. If you did you would never… You used me. You lied to me. You pretended to care about me when all the time—'

'Tilly, no!'

'So it's not true? You're not this James Connaught?'

Silas's mouth compressed. Why the hell hadn't he followed his own instinct and his heart and told Tilly the truth earlier? 'I *do* write as James Connaught, yes.'

'And you also moonlight as an out-of-work-actor, hiring yourself out as an escort?'

The bitterness in Tilly's voice made him want to hold her as tightly as he could, until he had absorbed her pain into himself.

'No,' he told her quietly. 'It was my half-brother Joe who was supposed to come here with you. He asked me to stand in for him because he'd had an accident. At first I refused, but then when he mentioned Art—'

'You changed your mind.'

It wasn't in Silas's nature to lie, especially not to someone who was as important to him as Tilly. 'Yes.'

'And when you accused me of hiring you for sex you were just testing the water, were you? Seeing how far you'd have to go to get what you wanted?'

'That had nothing to do with my hope that I could get closer to Art. I was concerned for Joe. He's young and impressionable, and I wasn't convinced that the outfit he was working for was as above board as he claimed.'

Silas took a deep breath. What he had to say to her now was going to be the hardest thing he had ever had to say. He knew his honesty was going to hurt her, but the truth had to be told, so that they could move on from today.

'That first night here, when you threatened to end our "engagement", I did think in terms of establishing a relationship with you to ensure that I stayed.'

'You used me,' Tilly accused him, her voice flat and devoid of the emotion she was desperately afraid might overwhelm her. 'You deliberately lied to me, pretended that you were falling in love with me, when all the time I meant nothing to you.'

'No, that's not true.'

'You're right,' Tilly agreed. 'The fact that I was falling in love with you *was* quite important to you. After all, it made everything so much easier for you, didn't it?'

'That's not what I meant and you know it. You can't really believe that I would lie to you about loving you?'

'Why not? You've lied to me about everything else, haven't you? If you'd really cared about me, Silas, you would have told me the truth.'

'I intended to.'

Tilly laughed mirthlessly. 'When? After you'd got your story?'

'I should have told you. I admit that. But I felt… I didn't want to risk spoiling what was happening between us.'

Tilly could hardly bear to listen to him. The rawness in his voice made her eyes sting with fierce tears. He sounded so genuine, but of course he wasn't.

'As a matter of fact, I was about to tell you earlier— just before your mother interrupted us.'

Tilly frowned, her heart missing a heavy beat as it clung desperately to the fragile hope of his words. She remembered that he had been on the verge of saying something to her. She ached with longing to be able to believe him, but she wasn't going to let herself give in to that weakness. Not a second time. Her was using her, manipulating her vulnerable emotions, just as he had done all along.

'If you had really loved me you would have been honest with me right from the start.'

'Life is not like that, Tilly. I didn't know I was going to fall in love with you. I didn't even realise at first that was what I was doing. By the time I did, it was too late. You'd already accepted me as what you believed I was. And, rightly or wrongly, I felt that our love was still too new and too fragile to bear the weight of the kind of revelations I would have had to make. But that doesn't mean that I didn't plan to tell you everything. I did. I love you, Tilly, and you love me. Surely that love—our love—deserves a chance?'

Tilly gave him a cynical look. 'You really think you can go on lying to me, don't you? I may have been stupid enough to fall for your lies the first time round, Silas, but I'm not stupid enough to fall for them again now. You don't love me. And as for me loving you—the man I thought I loved doesn't exist, does he? You've still got the hire car here. I think the best thing you can do now is pack your things and leave. There's nothing here for you now.'

Silas felt the shock of her rejection slicing through him, snapping the chain with which he had been leashing his own emotions. 'Nothing? Then what exactly is *this*, then?' he demanded.

He was still holding her wrist, and so he was able to catch her off balance enough to drag her into his arms and then cover the furious protest she made with the fierce heat of his mouth.

She wanted to resist him. She fought to do so. But something stronger than pride or pain was wrenching control of her responses from her, so that instead of closing into a tight, hard line against him her lips were opening under his, to return the full fury of his anguished passion. Somehow it was as though this was the only way she could show him the damage he had done—by violating the memory of what he had told her was love but what she now who knew was a lie.

This was all they had shared. Not love, not tenderness, and most certainly not the kind of almost spiritual emotional bond she had so stupidly deluded herself into thinking they had. Just this ferally savage physical need, poisoned with bitterness and deceit. Let it have its way, then; let it take her. Let it take them both and destroy itself as it did so, Tilly decided furiously.

Somehow he would break down Tilly's anger and resistance. Somehow he would find the right way to show her that their love was strong enough to survive the damage he had inflicted on it and on her. He had to find it. Because he couldn't endure the thought of losing her, Silas acknowledged as he tried to gentle the fierceness of his need and bring tenderness back into their intimacy.

He wanted to take Tilly and show her everything he felt—his remorse and regret, his pain and despair, his sorrow that he had hurt her and his reasons for having done so. He wanted to hold her in his arms, body to body, skin to skin, and to kiss the tears from her eyes. He wanted to beg for her forgiveness and to heal the wounds he had inflicted with the salve of his true love. He wanted to wipe away everything that had gone wrong and give them a fresh start. But most of all he wanted her to know that his love for her was hers for ever.

And this wasn't the way to show her that, Silas warned himself as he fought against succumbing to the drug of his own need. If he took her now, like this, when she was acting out of anger and bitterness, he would be damaging them both. He knew that, and yet at the same time he ached to take the chance that somehow he could mend things between them by showing her physically how much she meant to him.

The fire was dying out of her anger now, leaving behind a void that was filling with pain. Tilly shivered in Silas's hold.

'Tilly…'

'Just go, Silas. Please, just go.'

CHAPTER THIRTEEN

'SILAS rang again this morning.'

Tilly heard her father's words but she didn't give any sign. It was over two months since she had last seen Silas. Two months during which he had attempted with relentless determination to make contact with her, and she had refused to let him with equal determination.

He had even tracked her down here, to her father's farm in Dorset, where she had come for a much-needed break not so much from her job as from Silas himself, and the ghost of their love.

'He's sent you this,' her father continued, holding out to her a large A4-sized parcel. 'It's the typescript for his book. He asked me to tell you that he wants you to be the first to read it.'

Tilly's mouth compressed. Somehow or other Silas seemed to have managed to persuade her father to act as his supporter, even though she had told her father what he had done.

'Tilly, I know what he did was very wrong, but why don't you give him a chance to explain and make amends?'

'Why should I?'

'Do you really need me to tell you that?' Her father asked dryly. 'You still love him, no matter how much you might try to convince yourself that you don't, and from what he's said to me he certainly loves you.'

'It's because of what he did that Art broke off his engagement to Ma,' Tilly pointed out.

Her father raised his eyebrows. 'If you ask me, your mother had a lucky escape. *She* certainly seems to think so. And she hasn't lost much time in finding someone to replace Art, has she?'

Tilly gave a small uncomfortable wriggle. It was true that her mother was now blissfully in love with a new man—and, although Tilly wasn't about to say so to her father, Annabelle too had been doing her utmost to persuade Tilly to give Silas a second chance.

'We're going out now,' her father said. 'See you later.'

Tilly was trying very hard not to look at the manuscript on the table in front of her. She didn't even know why she had removed the packaging. But she had, and now, like Pandora with the lid of the box lifted, she was unable to control her own curiosity to see what lay inside.

Pinned to the first page of the manuscript was a letter addressed to her. She wasn't going to read it. She was going to tear it up, as she had all the other letters Silas had sent her. But somehow her fingers weren't obeying her brain, because the letter was open and unfolded, and Silas's firm, masculine handwriting was dancing on the page in front of her through the sudden surge of tears filming her eyes.

How could she still love a man who had already

shown her so devastatingly that his career would always come first and that in order for it to do so he was prepared to lie to her? What kind of future would they have if she gave in and let Silas back into her life? Did she really need to ask herself that? It would be a future in which she and their children could never completely trust in Silas's love and honesty; a future in which they could never totally rely on him to be there for them. The future, in fact, that she had always feared.

Her fingers trembled as she held the letter. Why bother to add to her own pain by reading it? But it was too late.

I won't write to you yet again of my love for you. Love is, or should be, two halves of one whole, Tilly. I know my own half for what it is, but only you know yours. I had thought—mistakenly, perhaps—that your half matched mine in its absoluteness and constancy. Perhaps the message you want to send me via your silence is not that you refuse to forgive me or accept my explanations for my errors, but rather that you yourself have had second thoughts and have welcomed the chance to act on them.

As she read what he had written Tilly could hear him speaking the words as clearly as though he were standing next to her. She closed her eyes and let the pain take her.
Silas.
She still loved him. She knew that. Just as she knew that she always would. She opened her eyes and continued to read.

If that is so, then that is your right, and I cannot persuade you otherwise, but so far as my own feelings are concerned my love for you exists as truly as it always has done and always will. Meeting you has had a profound effect on me in more ways than one. If you read this manuscript then I hope you will see and understand.

Tilly turned over the first page. On the second there was a brief dedication which read *For my mother*.

She read for so long that her body felt stiff and cramped, but she was so engrossed in what she was reading that she hadn't been able to drag herself away, Tilly admitted.

She had expected Silas's book to be about the oil industry—which in some respects it was. But only some. What it told was the story of his mother, and those like her, who had crusaded against the tyranny of materialism over human life and the environment. What she'd read compelled her to go on reading, and moved her immensely. Now she had almost reached the end, and as she turned the final page of the penultimate chapter she found an envelope pinned to the manuscript.

It was addressed to her.

Inside she found a brief note, and another envelope.

If you have read this far then you will know by now that I decided against writing about Jay Byerly and have written instead about my mother's life and work. I made that decision because of you,

Tilly. I was wrong not to tell you right from the first who I was and why I took Joe's place. I love you, and I'd like the chance to prove my love to you if you will give it to me. In the envelope is a ticket. If you choose to give me a chance then please use it. If you choose not to—if you don't, after all, love me enough to accept me with my faults and flaws—then I won't bother you again.

Did Silas really dare to question her love for him? Angrily, Tilly opened the second envelope. It contained an air ticket to Madrid.

Very carefully she put it to one side, and went back to the manuscript. When she read Silas's spare description of his mother's death in an accident that should never have happened, and *would* never have happened if it hadn't been for the actions of Jay Byerly, Tilly had to stop reading because her tears had blurred the print so badly.

At the end of the chapter Silas had written:

The very best gift my mother gave me was her love for me; the legacy she left me was to learn to grow enough to understand that love achieves more than bitterness or resentment. It was her love for her fellow man that prompted her to give so much to others, and it is my love for one very special person that has led me to write about the love that motivated my mother rather than my own bitterness at the manner of her death.

And then, underneath:

You are that woman, Tilly. Just as my mother's ring fitted you perfectly, I would like to think that in one way she was responsible for bringing you, the woman who fits me so perfectly, into my life and my heart. Both of them are empty without you.

She was a fool for doing this. It was crazy. No, Tilly corrected herself as she walked through the Arrivals hall and blinked in the sharp Spanish spring sunshine. *She* was crazy. What was the point of doing this? It was over between her and Silas. So over that there hadn't been a single night since they had been apart when she had not fallen asleep thinking about him, nor a single day that hadn't been shadowed by her bitterness and pain? Just how over was that, exactly? Tilly derided herself.

She could see a small plump Spaniard, holding up a placard bearing her name.

'I am José,' he informed her cheerfully. 'I am your driver. You have just the one bag?'

'Just the one,' Tilly agreed. She had no idea what Silas was planning, and even less why she should be travelling like this—on trust and hope and something that came perilously close to the love she had spent the last few weeks furiously denying existed.

There was no snow in Madrid, but as they began to climb Tilly could see where it still lay across the mountains, and she could see too where their route was taking them. Her heart thudded into her chest wall, and she gave in to the ache inside her that contained longing as well as pain.

It was no real surprise when they finally reached Segovia, and José brought the car to a halt outside the hotel where she had stayed with Silas.

A smiling receptionist welcomed her, and in no time at all she was being shown up to the familiar suite.

The only thing that did surprise her was that it was empty and there was no sign of Silas. Surprised her or disappointed her?

She looked out of the window and down into the street below. On some impulse she didn't want to answer to she had brought with her the black dress she had bought here. She heard the outer door to the suite open and she turned round.

Silas! The bones in his face were surely more prominent, and he wore something in the aura he carried with him that looked like shadowed pain.

'All this is a bit dramatic, isn't it?' she asked, striving to sound cool and self-possessed.

'It wasn't intended to be.'

'No? Then what *was* it intended to be?' she challenged him.

'A hope that although it isn't possible to physically turn back time, I can at least show you how much I wish that I could do so.'

It had been here that they had finally made love, and she had given herself to him in love and in hope and with trust and belief. And now, with him standing here in front of her, her body and her emotions were filled with the memory of all that they had shared before reality had destroyed her dreams.

'When would you turn back time to? The moment you rejected Cissie-Rose's advances? After all, she could have helped you so much more than I did.'

'She could have. But by that stage you had become far more important to me than my book—even though I didn't have the wit to admit that to myself. No. I'd turn it back to the time before we made love, when I held you in my arms, knowing that we would do so. To when I should have told you the truth but was too afraid of spoiling things between us. Perhaps I sensed then more strongly than you did yourself that you already had doubts about your own feelings.'

Tilly couldn't answer him. While his challenge to her in his letter had shocked and angered her, she was honest enough to know that there was an element of truth in it.

'I'd spent so long planning to reveal Jay Byerly and his coterie of associates for what they were because of my mother that I felt honour-bound to stick to my plan—even though I knew I would have to deceive you. I couldn't see then that I would honour my mother's memory far more positively by writing about what she believed in rather than denouncing those who had stood against those beliefs. I hope I have done her justice.'

'You have,' Tilly told him softly. 'No one could read your book and not be moved by it, Silas. If you had told me from the first…'

'I'd planned to tell you once we were back in London, when you wouldn't be under so much pressure from conflicting interests.'

'What about your own conflict of interests?' Tilly asked him quietly. 'How can you expect me ever to feel that the emotional security of our relationship and our children will be safe in your hands, Silas, when I've already witnessed you lying to me for the sake of your ambitions?'

'It wasn't like that. I had committed to that ambition before I met you and fell in love with you, and I had already abandoned my commitment to it because of my love for you—even though I didn't get the opportunity to tell you that. You and our four children will always come first with me, Tilly.'

'Our *what*?'

Tilly watched, fascinated, to see a faint tide of colour creeping along Silas's jawline.

'That was when I knew how much you meant to me. When you told me about your father's farm and out of nowhere I started visualising you living in the country with four children—our children.'

'I've always thought that four children would be the ideal family,' Tilly told him shakily.

'You'll have to marry me to get them. And you'll have to love me and let me love you—and them—for always.'

Just being with him and listening to him was melting away all her stubborn resistance. Reading Silas's book had already filled her with a tide of emotion that had swept away everything that had dammed up her love and turned it sour and bitter with anger and resentment. And now…

'Silas…' she began unsteadily.

'Don't look at me like that,' he warned her. 'Because if you do, then I will have to do this…'

How could she ever have convinced herself that she could live without him, when here in his arms was the only place she really wanted to be?

'Silas,' she said again, but this time she was whispering his name eagerly and happily against his lips, and letting him take the aching sigh of her breath from her as he kissed her.

An hour later, lying curled up next to Silas in the warmth of the bed where he had just shown her how much he missed her, and promised her that their future together would be everything she wanted it to be, Silas lifted Tilly's left hand to his lips, kissing the finger on which he had replaced his mother's ring.

'Just promise me one thing?' he said.

'What?' Tilly asked.

'That you won't tell me that you want to get married on New Year's Eve in a castle in Spain. Because there is no way I can bear to wait that long.'

'Neither can I,' Tilly admitted, laughing. And then she stopped laughing as Silas bent his head to kiss her.

MILLS & BOON®
Live the emotion

1206/01b

Modern
romance™

THE MILLIONAIRE'S PREGNANT WIFE
by Sandra Field

Kelsey North finally has her freedom back – and she plans to enjoy it! So when millionaire Luke Griffin offers to take her to the Bahamas and fulfil all her fantasies, Kelsey can't say no… But when their passion leads to pregnancy, Luke has only one solution – marriage!

THE GREEK'S CONVENIENT MISTRESS by Annie West

Sophie Patterson is shocked when Costas Palamidis turns up on her doorstep. Costas's little girl's life is in danger and Sophie is the only person who can help… Soon Sophie finds herself falling for Costas…but can she ever be more than his mistress?

CHOSEN AS THE FRENCHMAN'S BRIDE
by Abby Green

Tall, bronzed Xavier Salgado-Lezille isn't a man a girl can easily say no to. Jane Vaughn tries to play it cool, but she is inexperienced…and a virgin. Falling in love isn't part of the plan…neither is discovering she is pregnant once she's home and the affair is over…

THE ITALIAN BILLIONAIRE'S VIRGIN
by Christina Hollis

Gorgeous, ruthless Antonio Michaeli-Isola is determined to reclaim his birthright and make the Tuscan palace Larissa has just inherited his own! If that means seducing and discarding her, then so be it. But Larissa is hiding a secret… Will Antonio realise before it is too late?

On sale 5th January 2007

*Available at WHSmith, Tesco, ASDA, Borders, Eason,
Sainsbury's and most bookshops*

www.millsandboon.co.uk

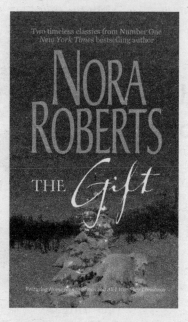

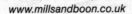

FREE!

4 Books

and a surprise gift!

We would like to take this opportunity to thank you for reading this Mills & Boon® book by offering you the chance to take FOUR more specially selected titles from the Modern Romance™ series absolutely FREE! We're also making this offer to introduce you to the benefits of the Mills & Boon® Reader Service™—

- ★ **FREE home delivery**
- ★ **FREE gifts and competitions**
- ★ **FREE monthly Newsletter**
- ★ **Exclusive Reader Service offers**
- ★ **Books available before they're in the shops**

Accepting these FREE books and gift places you under no obligation to buy, you may cancel at any time, even after receiving your free shipment. Simply complete your details below and return the entire page to the address below. You don't even need a stamp!

YES! Please send me 4 free Modern Romance books and a surprise gift. I understand that unless you hear from me, I will receive 6 superb new titles every month for just £2.80 each, postage and packing free. I am under no obligation to purchase any books and may cancel my subscription at any time. The free books and gift will be mine to keep in any case.

P6ZEF

Ms/Mrs/Miss/Mr ....Initials ....
                  BLOCK CAPITALS PLEASE
Surname ....
Address ....

....

....Postcode ....

Send this whole page to:
UK: FREEPOST CN81, Croydon, CR9 3WZ